TO THE
FAR CORNERS

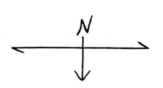

OTHER WORK BY RED CLOUD WOLVERTON

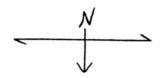

"STAGECOACH 76"
(THE LAST STAGE WEST FROM ST. JO)

"THE DEVIL'S GARDEN"
(short story published in TALES FROM
COWBOY COUNTRY compilation)

"JIMMYKANE"
(short story published in GOOD MEDICINE compilation)

Regular writer/contributor to COWBOY MAGAZINE

TO THE
FAR CORNERS

BY

'RED CLOUD' WOLVERTON

ILLUSTRATED BY MARGERY WOLVERTON

Note for Librarians: A cataloguing record for this book is available from Library and Archives Canada at www.collectionscanada.ca/amicus/index-e.html
ISBN 1-4120-8338-9

Printed in Victoria, BC, Canada. Printed on paper with minimum 30% recycled fibre. Trafford's print shop runs on "green energy" from solar, wind and other environmentally-friendly power sources.

Offices in Canada, USA, Ireland and UK

Book sales for North America and international:
Trafford Publishing, 6E–2333 Government St.,
Victoria, BC V8T 4P4 CANADA
phone 250 383 6864 (toll-free 1 888 232 4444)
fax 250 383 6804; email to orders@trafford.com
Book sales in Europe:
Trafford Publishing (UK) Limited, 9 Park End Street, 2nd Floor
Oxford, UK OX1 1HH UNITED KINGDOM
phone 44 (0)1865 722 113 (local rate 0845 230 9601)
facsimile 44 (0)1865 722 868; info.uk@trafford.com
Order online at:
trafford.com/06-0093

10 9 8 7 6 5

CONTENTS

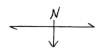

ILLUSTRATIONS

There were horses in the air going end over end, and cows being slammed everywhere.

- page - 28

"Red, I'd like to buy you a drink and wish you Merry Christmas. This is Christmas Eve."

- page - 52

I guess we were quite a sight to them, with our big sombreros, silk neck scarves, and buckskin vests.

- page - 60

As I felt him tumbling under me, I pulled my knees up under me and tried to go with the tumble, rolling as far out of his way as possible.

- page - 80

It was so dark, and the trail down the slope was so steep, that I walked and led my horse quite a ways.

- page - 97

We stood there toe to toe, and traded slugs, with neither one of us trying to block the other's blows, for ages, it seemed like.

- page - 116

Once in awhile, when I'd get a view of his head, I'd take a swipe at it, but most of the time, I couldn't keep track of where his head was.

- page - 133

Applesauce stood there with his head cocked around to the side, watching me for a minute; then straightened out and slightly arching his neck, raised his head in the air.

- page - 164

We were again shackled with our hands behind our backs, this time around the posts of a "lick log", or very stout hitch rail.

- page - 185

I spent many days sitting there by that headstone, during the next few months.

- page - 197

"My God, Sandy, I've found you at last!"

- page - 207

A big full, yellow moon was flooding down on the prettiest, homiest-looking ranch headquarters I could ever imagine.

- page - 223

I'd build to them, ride right into their midst, and rope a good stout young one, and the battle would be on.

- page - 228

As far as my office is concerned, the case is closed.

- page - 246

To my wife,

I have ridden many a bucking horse, and been piled by more than I care to mention. I've chased cattle in the mountains of Colorado, trailed them across the desert in Arizona, and roped them out of boggy marshes in Oregon. I've driven chuckwagons, freight wagons, and stagecoaches; and can drive six head in most any wild way; but I can't play a typewriter.

I would like to share my credit for this work with my wonderful wife Margery, for painstakingly wading through my pages of hand scribbled manuscript and putting it in ledgible form.

"Red"

PREFACE

For years, I thought of writing a western novel. Plot after plot was discarded. I didn't want a run-of-the-mill type of story; it had to be something special.

Then in the winter of 1975, for three nights in a row, I dreamed the same horrifying nightmare. When I awoke after the third time, I knew this was the basis for my story. All I had to do then was figure how my hero came to get into his predicament; and how he handled the events afterwards. For me that was simple.

I had a lifetime of working on the big ranches in the West; days, weeks, months, and years of bucking horses, stampeding cattle, and runaway teams which I could draw on. I had taken part in most of the predicaments, and knew many a cowboy in other wild escapades. I simply wrote down a few of those wild times, as the story developed. I hope you will enjoy reading about it, as much as I have enjoyed writing about "my younger days."

Sincerely,

Red Cloud

Chapter I

JUSTIFIABLE HOMICIDE?

I waited for the explosion. Suddenly it came, with smoke and rocks belching into the air from the crevice in the rocks. The ground under my feet trembled as I watched from the distance. If there were any pieces of body left after that; they wouldn't be identifiable.

"There, you murderous, filthy cabron! It's over. It's done with. Let's see you come back to life now!"

I turned to get my horse. There, standing about two hundred yards away, was a second horse. Annabelle! Oh, my God!

Riding slowly up to her, coiling my rope, I could see the sickness in her; the utter disgust and loathing. I knew immediately that she had watched the whole thing. She could not see, and probably would never know, the heartache her appearance had given me. I couldn't tell her. I had to play it straight with her, the way I'd always done.

"Annabelle, I know you've just watched a terrible thing. I can see the horror in your face that your father could commit such a merciless act as the killing you just watched. You are thinking it's your duty to report me to the law, and you are wondering how you can do that to me, your father. I'm proud you have that attitude, as that is the way I've tried to raise you, good and honest and true. What you have just seen makes a mockery of all the years I've tried to teach you right and patience and understanding.

This killing is "murder" in your mind —merciless, mutilating, and malicious. You can't even imagine why any person would do

what I just did. In my mind, it was an extermination. It settles the score for a lifetime of hunting. If you will come back to the ranch with me, I'll tell you that story. Afterwards, if you are still of a mind to, you can call the sheriff; and I'll go along willingly."

Without a word, she turned and followed me. Her face was calm, but stern. She averted her eyes. She couldn't stand to look at me.

We put up the horses in silence. I walked on to the house, calling for Monte to come to the den. Without a word, Annabelle followed slowly. She looked questioningly at Monte as she came in and closed the door; but Monte was watching me, not knowing what had happened, but quick to sense the feeling of tension between us.

I walked over to the old safe, opened it, and took out an old manuscript. With it in my hand, I turned to face the two women. Knowing Monte would soon understand without explanation, I said to Annabelle, "The thing I have just destroyed caused your mother to die the most humiliating death a woman could possibly die of. She was degraded and humiliated beyond all endurance; but she was strong, and I'm sure she wouldn't have died even then, except she saw me standing there all shot to pieces, with blood running down my naked chest. I became so weak I could stand no longer. I fell to the ground beside her and found her hand. I can still see her try to smile at me as I gently kissed her lips before I passed out. When I came to, she was dead.

No, Annabelle, I'm not talking about Monte, here; the sweet, gentle woman you have believed to be your mother all your life. Monte is your foster mother. She has wanted to tell you so many time, but the time wasn't right. She doesn't know all the story which I am about to tell you. She has believed in me all these years, while I was waiting for the terrible score to be settled; afraid to tell you she was not your real mother because it could have changed the finish here today.

I had one very close dear friend. Long ago, I promised him that when the time came to tell the story, I would go way back to the beginning and leave nothing out. After you know the whole thing, maybe you will change you mind about what you saw today. In these pages is a complete account of everything that happened."

I handed them to Monte, saying, **"You know nothing about my younger years. Read it aloud for all of us. It will answer all the questions you have lived with for so long."**

With a gentle smile for me, she took the faded pages and softly began to read.

"I was raised as an orphan, shuffled from one orphanage to another, until at a tender age during the depression, I was finally booted out on my own.

The day that good old Dad Worthington found me surely must have saved my life. I was broke, half scared, and hadn't eaten hardly anything for several days. Life was looking pretty miserable to a punk of a kid that day. Then this big cowboy came by where I was sitting in a store window all drawed up. I can still hear him saying to me, "Hey Red Head, come help me tote this big box out to my wagon. Then we'll go see if we can't find a restaurant that's open somewhere."

By the time we'd got the wagon loaded, I was feeling better, but I was sure getting hungry and weak. That cowboy didn't back up a bit though. He took me to a little place and ordered for both of us. Then he ordered for me again. I was so full I could hardly walk out of the joint.

As we were going back up the street, he says to me, "You got a home somewheres, or folks, Red?"

It sort of hurt to come out with it, but I finally said I was an orphan.

When we got back to the wagon, he says, "If you can drive that team, you can go out to the ranch with me."

I didn't know much about driving, but I had done it a few times. I replied, "Betcha I can handle them."

That started my ranch life. I was only about fourteen then, but big for my age, and able to stand lots of work. I started in as flunky, and worked up to the horse wrangler job. I finally "graduated" as a full fledged top hand cowboy by the time I was eighteen years old. That

17

big cowboy, Dad Worthington, was a good man and a top hand. He showed me how to do lots of things in the four years I stayed there.

I guess I never would have left his ranch, but some older fellow got jealous of me and started a quarrel. I was afraid I'd shoot him if I stuck around. Rather than to do that, I just saddled my horse and left.

Times were pretty rough. After four years work, all I had was my horse and saddle, bedroll, a few clothes, and an old 45 six-shooter.

I didn't buy the horse. The first winter I worked for Worthington, he had me in a camp, away from headquarters, where we'd stacked hay the previous summer. I had four head of work horses, a hay wagon, a pitchfork, and a bunch of old cows to feed. Along in January, after several real bad days of blizzard, I finally was able to get out to feed again. The wind and snow had blowed down the valley something awful, and had drifted all the cattle way down to the lower end where there was some protection. I had a hard time getting the wagon into the stack yard, and a worse one forking the hay. If I hadn't had four head of horses to pull my load, I couldn't have made it through the drifts. As it was, I had to go way around several places where the snow had drifted too deep to go through. I thought I saw something in one snow-clogged draw as I was working my way around the end of it. I went to check to see what it was. There was a young horse in pretty bad shape. Apparently he had been driven by the blinding storm and had fallen in the wash in deep snow. He was weak, thin, scared, and pretty helpless. I see he'd need some help to get out of his fix; so I decided to feed him some hay, and then see if I could get him out of the wash after feeding the cows.

I didn't have much of a rope with me; so it was quite a struggle to get the wagon down close enough to tie onto his neck. I thought I was going to pull his head off before he finally came out of the hole. He finally got to his feet after I drug him up on solid ground. He was scared to death and wanted to fight and pull back, but he was too weak to put up much of a battle. I looked him over pretty good and could see he wasn't branded. He looked like he must be about a two year old. He was awful thin, but he had a good frame; so I decided to see if I could get him back to my camp. He sure wasn't broke to lead, but was too weak to struggle much. My horses would drag him tied to the wagon with no trouble, but I tried not to be too rough on him. It was almost night, and I was about frozen when we finally got back into the corral. I pulled the wagon up by my little barn, where there was shelter, and just left this gray horse tied, and throwed him some feed. I figured I just as well halter break and gentle him, since I had him caught.

I named that poor horse right there—scared, half starved, with chunks of ice hanging from his body, mane, and tail.

"Goodnight, Blizzard," I says, "I'll see you in the morning."

We had a good time there, the rest of that winter. My four work horses, the grey horse, and myself; our cows, the coyotes, and cold winter blizzards one after another. By the time spring came around, and a crew came out from headquarters to check on me and move the cows, I had Blizzard as gentle as a dog. I'd put a little fat on his ribs, and had even gotten him broke to ride bareback. I didn't have a saddle then. When Mr. Worthington saw my horse and heard my story, he said that I just as well keep him for my own; especially since he was unbranded. He'd probably drifted out of some mustang band.

Blizzard and I were both young. It's a wonder I didn't spoil him, but the outfit had some real good cowboys, and one named Long Tom sorta took a liking to me I guess. Anyway, he gave me an old saddle that he had extra, and spent a lot of time teaching me how to school my horse. By the time I left that outfit, Blizzard was getting to be a good cowhorse; and I guess I had become a fair hand for an eighteen year old.

There had been many cowboys from all over the West drift into and away from that ranch in the four years I was there. I'd never grown tired of listening to their tales of other ranges and cow outfits. Many the time, I thought of drifting to those wonderful far off places; but I'd never had the excuse before. Now I was free and able to ride wherever I pleased. New Mexico had a magic sound to my ears in those days' so that's where I headed — toward a little old cowtown I'd heard of way out in the middle of nowhere.

Traveling wasn't too difficult in the cow ranges then. You could usually drift from one line camp to another in a day's ride. There'd generally be some coffee and beans or a little canned goods in most of the camps. Some days weren't so good though. I wouldn't find a camp or ranch. That's when I learned to skin a porcupine. They are pretty good eating, roasted over a good juniper or cedar fire. You lay them on their back, split the hide down the belly; then start rolling it back to each side so as to keep the quills inside.

I'd ridden quite a ways across New Mexico and was feeling pretty low. I'd asked several outfits for a job, but it was the wrong time of the year, and nobody was hiring. I finally decided to work up into some country where there was game and see if I could find a vacant line camp to hole up in until I could find a job.

It was beautiful country I was heading into, with high snowcapped mountains in the distance. There was lots of meadow parks, timber, and running water. I'd been seeing quite a bit of game sign, and decided all I needed was a camp; then I wouldn't care if I found a job or not.

I was following a winding meadow up the country, when I heard a noise that sounded like a horse bucking or running hard. About that time, here pops this big buckskin horse out from behind a grove of jackpine. Boy, he was really pawing his head. He was jumping high and crooked, and it sure looked like he was dropping one shoulder and falling to the side each time he hit the ground. His rider was still with him when they came in sight, but I could see in an instant he was in real trouble.

I jumped Blizzard ahead as fast as I could, but I knew I wouldn't get to that wild chunk of exploding horse flesh in time to help the rider. The best I figured I could do was to jerk my rope down and build a loop as I closed in. I see the rider slung off and hit the ground in a splattering lump, just before I was within roping range; so I bored right in and threw my loop around old "Buck's" head, before he knew there was another horse in the country. I had a good clean neck

20

loop at the right angle, so took my turns and set Blizzard up.

We took Buck so much by surprise, he didn't even try to stop. I can still see him flipping over and being slammed to the ground. We knocked the stuffing right out of him. He must have laid there two or three minutes before he was able to scramble back to his feet.

After I got Buck gathered in, I turned to look for his rider. I could see right off, he wasn't a young man, and he was hurting. He raised up to a sitting position, but he was awful pale.

"I guess you're hurting pretty bad," I said, towing Buck toward him.

A nod, and "I'll make it," was about all the answer he could give. We didn't do much talking for awhile.

I got off my horse and unsaddled him. Then I unsaddled Buck and put my saddle in his middle. After I got both horses resaddled, I turned back to the old cowboy. He was all humped over and looked pretty beat.

I led Blizzard over to him. He was able to mount, but just barely. I didn't have to say anything to that horse; he sort of looked up at me and cocked an ear slightly forward. He seemed to be telling me that it was alright. He'd take care of the old boy; I didn't need to worry.

Buck snorted when I turned back to him. He also seemed to be able to read my mind. I was telling him, "Buck, old boy, try that on me, and I'll show you I'm not some old stove-up has-been. As a matter of fact, I just dare you to try that on me."

Those big tough northwest rough string horses had showed me lots of tricks. That "busting" on the end of my rope had probably helped change his mind too. Anyway, he didn't go to bucking when I stepped on him.

We rode quite a ways before my new friend got to feeling good enough to talk. His talk seemed a little pointed. It seemed he was asking a lot of questions of me; someone he'd just met, but I didn't take offense.

Finally we worked down to a larger valley with a good road running through it. The valley curved up ahead, and we were up fairly high on one side as we rounded the curve to where we could see up the country. It sure was a beautiful sight. There in the valley, nestled in a grove of trees on the far side, was a large ranch headquarters. I could see a big white house, and what I took for a bunkhouse, and cookshack, out a ways. Several barns and working corrals, with a few head of horses and cattle in them, finished the picture.

About that time, we could hear a dinner bell pealing across the valley. My friend was feeling good enough to sort of grin as he says, "It looks like we'll make it in time for supper if we hurry a mite. That is, if you're hungry."

Several times during our ride, I'd noticed this cowboy casting a strange speculative look at me, like he was about to say something; but then he'd seem to change his mind.

There was a big corral with the gate standing wide open as we rode up. It was a welcome sight. We'd just got through to the inside when my friend pulled up. Turning to me with a twinkle in his eye, he says, "You know what? I'd just give one pretty penny to see old Buck come uncorked with you, my boy!"

His statement called for an answer, but not in words. I swallowed my breath, as I sat there and looked him back straight in the eyes. I decided.

"Why not, Old Timer?"

I'd been wondering the same thing myself.

Reining Buck out of line of the old man, I slid way down in my riggin'. When I was clear of him, I poked the slack out in my reins. With a blood curdling squall, I reached up and hung my spurs in old Buck's shoulders. I didn't need to tell him twice what I was after. He was ready and willing, and met me head on.

I don't know how long we fought each other with every trick and counter trick in the book, but I do know I thought I'd made a mistake several times. Buck would all but have the riggin' jerked away from under me; then he'd miss a lick, and I'd get back in time with him. He started out bucking high and ahead, and hitting the ground like a pile driver; then he'd drop one shoulder and feint to one side, like I thought he'd been doing earlier in the day. That wasn't doing the job, so he started jumping ahead and sunfishing a couple times. He did it so hard and fast, I was sure I was looking off over his rump. I was just about to lose him, but then he slowed down a bit, and I got caught up again. I'll say one thing. That buckskin horse knew lots of tricks, and he was trying them all on me. One sunfish jump ended with his four feet out horizontal, his whole body was shaking like the way a dog shakes his head and body when he has dived in and grabbed a diamondback in it's mouth, and is shaking it to death.

Next, he threw a wrinkle at me I'd only been through once before. He drove into the ground on stiff front legs; then started bucking backwards. I think he might have lost me there, as I was getting way over forwards, when he bucked back into the corral fence. That sort of broke his confidence for he started forward again, but just in big, straight, slow jumps.

I'd quit spurring him a long time ago, except just to grab ahead. He bucked half way across the corral and finally stopped, all humped up with his head hanging down.

We sat there like that, both of us puffing so hard our ribs were about to bust; so weak we could hardly hang on.

Finally I pulled up gently on the reins and says, "Come on Buck, it's all over. Let's be friends."

I nudged him gently in the side. He sort of cocked his head slightly and looked at me for an instant with held breath. Letting it out in a rush, he walked off gently across the corral toward the barn.

I'd been so busy with Buck, I hadn't had the chance to look around until now. There on the fence was the cook and the whole cowboy crew. Nobody was talking, but I could see from the look on their faces, they all admired the performance they'd just seen; both Buck's and mine.

As I rode up to the gate, the cook stepped down off the fence. Looking behind me toward the old cowboy, he says, "Shake a leg, Boss. Supper's getting cold."

I was sure taken by surprise. That old cowboy was the boss of this good looking crew and ranch.

Then the cook turns to me and says, "There's a plate on the table for you too, 'Booger Red.'"

I told him, "Thanks much, I haven't had a square meal in quite awhile; but I'm so beat and shook up, I don't think I could get anything down for a little while."

The old cook turned back and looked square up at me with a real tough expression, like to let me know that maybe he was just the ranch cook; but that he was the undisputed boss of the cookshack on that ranch.

There wasn't a sound made by another man as the cook told me how things were on that ranch.

"Booger," he said, "We don't handfeed nobody around this outfit. You eat when it's put out in front of you, or you wait 'til the next meal."

I was about to tell him and his outfit to "go to Hell", get my grey horse, and get out of their way. Before I got my spiel going, the cook looked toward the boss and came out with, "I guess it wouldn't hurt to break that rule here tonight, would it Boss?"

Without waiting for an answer, he turned back to me and said, "There shore will be a big plate of food on the table for you, Red, when you feel like tying into it."

I was accepted into that ranch and crew right then and there. It was a good ranch, crew, and boss to tie in with.

The next morning after breakfast, I was moseying toward the corral and my horse. The boss called to me from where he was sitting on his porch steps.

"Come over here a minute, Red."

As I walked up, he held up his hand in a friendly greeting and said, "Muchas Gracias for helping me out yesterday."

I don't remember if I answered or not. It kind of embarrassed me to be thanked for doing something any other cowboy would have done.

"Red," he said, "I've got a whole pasture full of half brothers to that buckskin horse you rode in here yesterday. I was wondering if you'd be interested in snapping them out?"

I was so tickled, If I'd been a dog, I would have been wagging my tail.

"I can't think of a thing in the world I'd rather do," I managed to get out.

That ranch was just like coming home for me. I was accepted as a top hand by an older crew of cowboys that had spent their lives working cattle and horses.

I did a good job on that bunch of young broncs, and earned the respect of a good boss. I got a steady job out of the deal.

A couple of the colts bucked me off a few times, and a couple turned out to be pretty cranky horses; but by the time three or four months had rolled by, I had about twenty head of well-broke colts to turn over to the cowboy crew on the ranch.

One morning as I came riding by the Boss's house, he hollered at me and waved me over to where he was sunning hisself.

"Is that one of the last colts you tied up, Red?", he asked.

I nodded my head.

He went ahead to say it looked like I about had the bunch broke. I told him I thought they were handling pretty good. We sat there awhile making small talk. Finally he asked me if I'd ever handled work horses any. Of course, coming out of the Northwest, I'd had about as much work horse experience as any other kind. When I told him that, his face lit up. He told me he was glad to hear that. He said there was enough young horses in the work horse herd to make up a couple six-horse hitches that he'd like to get broke. He said I could borry some help from the cowboy crew whenever I started hooking them up, but he'd sure like to get them broke gentle if he could. He was tired of runaways and torn up equipment.

We picked out twelve head of four and five year old geldings -- six bays and six sorrels. They weren't real big as far as draft horses go, but I guess they weighed 1600 to 1800 pounds and were pretty stout.

I spent a couple days catching them and tying them up to halter break. In side of two weeks, I had them all coming along real well.

25

They were all leading good; the witch knots were combed out of their manes and tails; and I'd started working on their feet. I broke them all to drive individually with an open bridle and a couple lines before I started putting the harness on them.

I finally drove them in teams and got all six teams paired up the way I wanted. As fast as I got a team to handling in a big corral, driving them on foot; then I started taking them out around the rest of the ranch.

Always afoot, I drove those horses all over the ranch; around the buildings, by the chicken house, the hog house, around by the clothes lines; everywhere, before I started using them on a wagon.

Some of the old timers, when they'd see me, they'd just shake their heads. They'd never seen such goings on as what I was doing. They had all been used to hooking a green unbroke horse with a broke one on a big breaking wagon, and letting them run until they finally got to where you could handle them a little. That was a fast way to break horses to drive, but it took them a long time to get even half gentle.

I worked all my horses to the wagon in teams until they were handling to suit me. When I got two teams going good, I'd make a four horse hitch out of them.

The boss had told m, if I knew how to break them gentle, to take all the time I needed, to turn them out as two good six horse hitches.

After I got the fours going good and had driven them all over the ranch, I started putting the sixes together. I had driven a six-up in Oregon several times, and I was real anxious to get these two sixes together. I got one of the cowboys to work with me.

One man can get by with a big hitch by hisself if the horses are older and pretty well broke, but a fellow sure needs some help when he's just breaking them. Young horses can get into so many predicaments, you sometimes could use a whole crew to get things untangled.

One of the worst messes occurred one day after I had the horses working in six horse hitches. I'd driven them out on one of the main dirt roads hoping to see a little automobile traffic so they could get used to it.

A wiry little half Mex cowboy, Emanuel, was along, giving me a hand that day, and it was a good thing. We were jogging right on down the country when it all happened.

A car slipped right up behind us, from where, I don't know. It must have been coasting. All of a sudden there was a loud backfire and a roar, right beside us. The car was one of those Ford four door, two seated convertibles, and was full of young people. A Mexican fellow was driving. I think they were on some kind of excursion or sightseeing tour. Anyway, I always figured the first backfire was deliberate, and I know for sure the ones that followed were.

Of course, when that first blast went off, it scared the horses more than me; and I almost jumped off the wagon! Before you knew what happened, we were running as hard as six big Shires could go, and that's moving right along! I really wasn't driving them, but somehow I was able to hold them partway in line; until Emanuel could reach over and take the wheel lines out of my hands so he could help drive and try to hold them in.

I think we could have slowed them down a little, if the car wold have gone on by and left us alone. When the horses bolted and lit out, for a little ways we were traveling faster than the automobile. Finally the Mex got the car wound up and was almost up even with the swing team, when the thing exploded again. What little we'd been able to pull the horses down, was lost a whole lot quicker.

Its funny the way things happen sometimes. Above all the noise caused by the hitch running; harness jingling, wagon rattling, and that car roaring, I heard one of the gals in the car laugh and giggle and say, "Hey, look! He wants to race us!"

That was all the encouragement that Mex needed to stay in there and keep spooking our horses.

We would have turned off, but there was a ditch and a fence along our side of the road. There was no place to go.

We must have run for a mile or more like that, with that Mex just staying alongside, back just far enough to keep the horses all fired up.

If I'd had my pistol along with me that day, I'm sure this story would have ended a long time ago, right there on that road.

There were horses in the air going end over end, and cows being slammed everywhere.

In all that confusion of trying to do something with those running horses, and shouting "Whoa-ahhh!'" and at the same breath swearing at the Mex to get that damn car back, I did see a beautiful sight; one that I've remembered all my life, and that I can still see here today. In the back seat of that touring car was a young girl with the beautifulest head of red hair flowing in the breeze, that I had ever seen. It was several years before an accident brought us together again, and quite awhile after that, before I ever figured out that she was the girl in the back of that car.

The last time I saw her that day, came almost to being the last time I ever saw anything.

We came pounding over a low raise in the road, and there a short ways ahead was a little bunch of cows. I think that Mex could have stopped, but he was probably afraid to. At the same time I saw the cows, I also spotted four cowboys coming in diagonally towards us on horses running as hard as they could go. I learned later they had heard and seen what was taking place, and were coming to our rescue.

The Mex poured the power to his automobile, skidding out around the cows. He pulled back onto the road ahead of them, about the same time we were piling into the little bunch.

The last glimpse I got of that red head of hair was mixed in with the picture of my lead team hitting those cows. Several had been laying down, and we'd dropped in on them so sudden-like, they only had time to start to scramble to their feet. There were horses in the air going end over end, and cows being slammed everywhere. In less than a couple seconds, we had all six horses in a pile on top of about that many cows.

When the wagon hit the pile of horses, it was stopped so quick that Emanuel and I were both shot through the air like we'd been hurled out of a catapult. I don't know how Emanuel landed, but I lit spread-eagled on a cow's back, clear out past the horses. I didn't stay there long. She jumped out from under me, and kicked me at the same time. I was rolling and tumbling, really out of balance. The lines had jerked out of my hands as I went flying over the horses, and that was enough to play "crack the whip" with me. For a little while after I finally hit the ground, I thought one of the horses was going to flop over on top of me. At the last minute, I guess his harness must have tightened up and jerked him back the other way, because he missed me.

By the time I was on my feet, the four cowboys had raced into our chaotic mess. The first I saw was one man sitting on his horse, trying to hold three excited horses so they didn't all get away.

That left five of us to jump in and start unbuckling harness to try to untangle the horses. Those cows that were mixed up in our hitch were fast becoming on the hook. Between swinging horns and flying hooves, it was a pretty hairy place to be for awhile.

We finally got everything untangled, and the cows all freed. Then we looked the outfit over. There didn't seem to be any animals hurt. All the cows ran off, and the horses were all standing OK. It took awhile to get all the harness untangled and buckled back together like it was supposed to be, and put back on the horses. We had a few broken straps, but nothing that we couldn't patch right there.

What really surprised me was that we hadn't broken the wagon tongue or the reach or swing pole. The way all six of those big horses piled up right on top of the tongue, it sure seemed strange we didn't break it out.

I was glad those four cowboys were there when we went to hook back up. It took all six of us to keep that hitch in hand for an hour or so after we got going again.

We missed our supper that night. Those four cowboys worked there on the same ranch, and they said they'd stay with me as long as I wanted them to, so we took quite a ride. We put about forty miles on those Shires that afternoon. When we got back to the ranch about dark, they had clean forgotten about their wild rampage with the thunder-snorting car.

A month or so later, the boss stopped me one morning. He had a stranger with him, and told me the man had come to look at the Shire hitch. If they suited him and he bought them, then he wanted to stay there several days to get acquainted with the hitch and drive them.

The boss went on to say that if the fellow bought the horses, that I could trail them down to his ranch in the lower part of Arizona. He had harness and wagons; he just needed the horses.

It didn't take that man long to fall in love with my Shires. Since the runaway, I'd really put in a lot of work on them, and they were handling real nice.

The Arizona rancher stayed for over a week, driving the Shires every day, and getting to know them. He would like to have trailed those horses back to his ranch with me, but he had to go on up into Colorado to buy some bulls. Anyhow, I set out with those guys by myself. I had my old grey horse, Blizzard, and it really felt good to take out on him again. I hadn't been riding him much for quite a spell.

I had a pack horse with me also. The boss told me to pick whatever horse I wanted, out of the extras; so I took that old son-of-a-gun, Buck, that I'd first run into on the ranch. I'd used him for a snub horse when I started that bunch of colts. He was cranky, but big and stout, and had really made a good snub horse.

I had all the company a cowboy could ever want; Blizzard, Buck, and the six Shires.

It took over a week to reach the Arizona ranch. The boss had laid out the route for me, marking ranches where I could put up for the night, and a couple places where I could buy more grain so I wouldn't need to pack anything but Buck. A couple times, he was fairly well loaded down with 200 pounds of grain and my camp outfit. It took a lot of grain to satisfy those Shires. They could eat ten or twelve pounds, and then look around for something more to eat.

I would have liked to stay down south there when I delivered the horses, and I was invited to; but I had a pretty good home up there in New Mexico. After resting my horses a couple days, and getting the ranch crew lined out with the Shires, and eating good cookhouse meals, I headed back north again.

I might have stayed down south, but for one thing. This was the first time I'd been off the ranch since I'd gone to work there. The ranch kept a commissary at the headquarters where you could get clothes, boots, and tobacco. There really was no need to go to town very often, unless you took to craving some of the city ways of living to let off a little steam.

On the way south, I'd come through a town that looked like it would be fun to spend a couple nights in. I had promised myself to do just that on the way back.

Blizzard, Buck, and I traveled a lot faster coming back by ourselves than we had going down. On the afternoon of the second day, we jogged into the town. It was quite a place. I pulled up and sat on Blizzard, studying Main Street. I could see the full length of it; a half mile or more of saloons, stores, and the courthouse square. The street was dirt; and there were horses, both harness and saddle, scattered the length of it between the cars and trucks. There wasn't much activity. Somewhere I could hear music floating by on a gentle breeze, probably coming out of one of the honky-tonks.

I sat there on Blizzard, anticipating the wonderful evening I was going to have.

First I had to find a place for my horses. Then I'd get me a hotel room. I had a little money; so next I'd shop around a little, maybe get me a whole new outfit. It had been a long time since I'd had more than one extra pair of levis. My boots and hat were both just about as worn out as they could get. After I got those new clothes, I'd stop by the barber shop and take a shower, put on the new clothes; then get a haircut and shave.

It'd be supper time by then. Next I might go see a movie. That would be a real treat. Then I might look in on the night spots. Who knows? The names on a couple of the joints looked pretty suspicious to me.

As I sat there soaking in the town, and wondering what to do with my horses, a big Irish fellow, carrying a lunch bucket, came by. He looked like he'd be the friendly type; so when he glanced up towards me, I spoke, just to pass the time of day. He stopped and leaned against a post, took out his pipe, and prepared it for a smoke.

We talked about the town; the restaurants, drygoods store, theater, and the honkys; everything I wanted to see. He'd lived there a long time and knew all the spots. Finally, when I asked him if he knew where I might put my horses up, he answered, "Yeah, I sure do. Why don't you just bring them on down to my house. I've got a good little pasture with grass and water in it, and I know your horses would like it."

That was settled. I had a good place for my horses, and a wide open town to see the sights in for the night. So what if it was 90 % Mexican? I had always enjoyed their company and got along good with them in the past.

I put up my horses and grained them good. Since I planned on buying new clothes in town, I discarded all the excess range clothes, my spurs, chaps, leather vest; and went uptown with about the same as the townspeople wore.

I had a hard time getting away from my new Irish friends, Larry and Mary O'Sullivan. We visited for awhile, and one thing led to another. When we got to talking about them living way down there in that Mexican town, Mary happened to say it was sure different from Plush, Oregon, where she'd grown up. When I told her I'd spent quite awhile out in that part of the high desert, it was like old friends meeting unexpected. They practically insisted I stay for supper , but I begged off by promising I'd show up for a 6 AM breakfast with them the next morning.

I didn't make it though. It was several years later before I got that breakfast.

The evening started like I planned, only instead of getting the hotel room, I went first to the general store. It was getting late. It sure felt good to be in town with a little spending money in my pocket.

I looked in at the barber shop on my way to the store. The barber said he'd wait for me, and he did have a shower stall in the back; so I really went whole hog in the Mercantile. New clothes from the ground up.

I visited with quite a few people that evening. On several occasions, when asked, I mentioned that I was only passing through; but luckily for me later on, I never said a thing about being ahorseback.

I had a good time. When I came out of the barber shop, I was starved to death; so I went into the hotel dining room and had a big fried chicken supper.

I could see the movie theater from where I sat. It opened up while I was eating; so afterwards I went over and saw Buck Jones in Red River Valley. I still hadn't rented a room and nobody in town knew my name.

When the movie was over, I felt more like looking in on some of the honkytonks than sitting in a hotel lobby.

I toured about half of whisky row before I found one I decided to go into.

I never drank very much at any time, but a cold bottle of beer is good to sip on to pass the time and see the sights. I climbed on a stool at the end of the bar and was about half way through my beer, when I became interested in a conversation going on at a table close by.

There were four Mexicans sitting there drinking tequila. What caught my attention was when I heard one of the fellows say, "Hey Rod, tell us about that wild race you and the college gals had with that freight team up north awhile back."

"Yeah, man, that was a riot.! You should have seen that dumb gringo when that first blast went off. I saw them up ahead quite a ways; so I speeded up real fast; then cut the motor off and coasted right up beside them without them ever knowing we were there. When I turned that motor back on, it really blasted out a good one. Boy, was that funny! That gringo driving those six big horses almost jumped off the wagon. Before he knew what was happening, those horses were going as hard as they could run. I drove right along by the side, and every time he'd start to slow his horses down, I'd turn that switch off and back on with another loud boom; and away they'd go again. And what was really funny was when we dropped over a hump in the road, and there was a herd of cows bedded down in the middle of it. Man, it was really something! I jabbed that old car and roared around the cows, and cut off the horses so they had to go right through the cows. Cows were going every which way, and horses piling end over end. Then the funniest sight was when that wagon hit that pile of horses. It stopped so quick that dumb gringo went flying through the air so hard I'll bet he's still rolling!"

It took a lot of control to set there and hear that story out. I'd promised myself that if I ever met that Mex, one of us wasn't going to walk away from the meeting. As he finished his story, and the four all busted out laughing, I slipped off the bar stool, turned around, stepped up to their table, and made my stand.

"You're damn wrong, chili burner," I snarled to the Mex called Rod. "And if you've got as much guts as you've got a big mouth, step outside with me, and we'll see how damn funny it was. If you're lacking guts, I'll just drag you outside!"

I was so totally thrilled at finding that Mex that I guess I wasn't watching the others. The first thing I knew, one of them had leaped out of his chair and lunged at me with a knife a foot long. I had really gotten careless; he had me pinned with his long knife stuck right through the skin of my throat!

As I was trying to back up to get away from the knife, this Mex says, "Stand still, Gringo, so I can cut your throat so my brother, the Sheriff can give us your fancy new clothes."

Since he had been drinking, I suddenly was sure he meant to do just what he said. The other three Mexicans were shouting encouragement to him as they came tearing out of their seats. Things didn't look good at all; that knife was still at my throat, just pricking the skin.

I don't know exactly what happened then, but as the Mex took a step ahead to keep up with my backing, his foot slipped. It caused him to drop down slightly; just enough to pull the knife a foot away from my throat. I didn't wait for an invitation. I picked up one of my fists from about hip pocket height and sent it crashing into that Mex's jaw.

All those months of jerking those big husky saddle broncs and work colts around had sure put a set of muscles in my arms and across my shoulders.

When I hit him, I put everything in it that I had. I knew when I connected with his jaw that he was out of the fight. I felt pretty sure it was more than just that; as there was an awful sound and feel to it, like bones being torn apart. I didn't have time to stop and mourn about hitting him too hard; those other three were all rushing toward me with knives that looked as long as swords.

Before the fracas had started, while I had been sitting at the bar, I had looked over the inside of the room pretty well, admiring the different pictures and articles hanging on the walls. One item that interested me quite a bit was a branding iron. Not that it was out of place here in a western bar, but because it was a typical Mexican iron; big and heavy, one that would really put a moonlight iron on a cow.

When I saw those fellas heading towards me with their flashing knives, I suddenly remembered that branding iron; and that it was right close behind me on the wall.

I just had time to turn, grab it and swing; but the way I was charged up, I believe I could have whipped six or eight of those guys. I took out lots of pent-up hatred there in the next few seconds. That's about all the time I had to spare; for, as I looked up, here came a whole swarm of Mexicans. There was a door with an "exit" sign over it, closer to me than they were; so I threw the branding iron at them and rushed through the door. It was a side exit that let me out between two buildings. I could hear the crowd swarming out into the street; so I turned and ran the other way.

I didn't know the town or where I was, but for the minute the best I could do was to get away from the main part of town.

Already I could hear sirens screaming and see police cars rushing every which way.

It took quite awhile slipping around in the dark to figure the lay of the town, and how to get back out to the O'Sullivans and my horses.

When I finally slipped up through their alley, I saw a movement that looked like a man near my horses. I had to stop and stand still a minute to keep from panicking; then I realized nobody in town but Larry and Mary knew I had ridden in ahorseback. If that was a man, it had to be Larry or else a thief trying to make off with something.

Deciding to chance it, I called softly, "Larry, is that you?"

"Yeah, Red, this is me. What in the heck have you been doing? The whole town's buzzing like a hornet's nest!"

"Larry, I run into a Mex I owed a debt to, and just paid it off with all the back interest. I think I might have broke one of the chili peppers' necks in the fracas. Are you with me Larry?"

"You bet, Red, I don't live down here because I love those boogers. It's my work that keeps me here."

"I better saddle up and light out then. Tell Mary goodby for me, will you?"

"Tell her yourself. She'll be here by the time we get your horses saddled up. She's putting some sandwiches and food in your pack for you now. She was sure you were the cause of all the commotion in town."

It didn't take long to get my horses ready to travel with Larry's help. Then Mary showed up with a load of food she could hardly pack. It sure made me wish I could have stayed there a few more days and visited with those good people.

That was almost like leaving home; riding away in the night and leaving those two friends standing there, arm in arm.

Larry had told me how to slip out of town and get away from the road blocks that were already set up, by staying away from the railroad tracks and picking up the trail that led off to the wild, rough, mountainous country up north.

I was "on the dodge", but I sure had settled one score that night.

Chapter II

ON THE DODGE

It was a lucky break for me nobody besides the O'Sullivans noticed me riding into town. The law assumed I'd driven in or come in on the train; so they had a pretty tight roadblock surrounding the village. From the commotion coming from up town, there was a large group of Mexicans spreading out and giving the town a thorough search, hunting for me.

There was a draw that came down out of the high country that wound through town, that I was able to get into and work my way back up into the hills. It was tough to have to leave town in that manner, but I certainly didn't want to get caught there.

By daylight, I'd put a good thirty miles between me and the town. I had grain for my horses; so when I located a pretty little secluded meadow with a small stream in it, I decided it would be a good place to stay until along towards evening.

After I got my horses staked out, I dug into the grubpack Mary had fixed for me. There were enough provisions to get by on for a week. Mary had even sent along a thermos jug of hot coffee, besides roast beef, cold fried chicken, and a sack full of biscuits and jerky. I found a high place where I could see the country behind me, made myself comfortable, ate, and then dropped off to sleep. I was sure no one had any idea where to look for me, but you never know. You can never totally relax when you're on the dodge.

I had been asleep a couple hours when the singing of the mountain jays, or maybe the lack of their singing, woke me up; to warn me that a human must be approaching. It's best to set still until you know what you're running from, before you start your running.

Presently, I spotted a couple fellows approaching ahorseback, with rifles in their arms. I almost panicked, with the desire to make a mad dash to get away; but something wasn't right.

One thing that worried me was if my horses became restless and caused a commotion, or if they started nickering. I guess they were tired enough not to get restless, as they didn't make any noise to give us away.

I could see the men weren't on my trail, and seemed to be watching something off to my left and below me. I spotted a large bull elk about the time these guys shot. It was a clean kill. I spent the rest of the day cat-napping and watching those guys dress out that elk and quarter it. Then they loaded it on their horses before they headed back away from where I was.

It didn't bother me that those two fellows were poaching that elk, but I didn't want them going back into civilization and reporting they'd run into a red-headed cowboy hid out in the hills. Someone would surely figure out who I was and be on my trail 'muy pronto".

It took several days to work my way back up across New Mexico and to the ranch. I rode mostly at night and stayed to rough country.

I knew the country good enough to ride the last day to the ranch in daylight. It was about four in the afternoon when I rode out on the ridge overlooking the headquarters.

It was a beautiful and sad sight. I had learned to love that ranch and crew in the months I'd been there. I knew I couldn't stay there anymore. It wouldn't be long before the law would think to look there for me, if they hadn't already done so.

I hated to leave without talking to the boss, but I couldn't. He'd want me to stay there and turn myself in; and then he'd put up a bond to keep me out of jail while we took the case to court.

I couldn't stand the thought of spending one day in jail. Guess I was part "mustang" myself.

After dark, I took Buck back down to the corral, then slipped around and got my good friend, Emmanuel Baejo, to come out, and and explained to him what had happened.

How I hated the thought of leaving that ranch. It had become "home" to me, and the boss and I had become good friends. But this was still New Mexico, and the only thing left for me to do was to drift.

Emmanuel was pleased when I told him about running into that Mex called "Rod", who had caused our wreck that time. He also was quite certain that it would only be a matter of time until the police located the ranch, looking for me. He agreed that it probably would be wise for me to disappear for awhile.

He would give the bad news of what had happened to me, to the boss in the morning.

Emmanuel thought I should take Buck with me. He knew the boss would approve. The thought of leaving without him was hard, as we'd learned to think a lot of each other after that first evening in the corral. We respected each other. He'd throwed every trick in the books at me and hadn't beaten me. He didn't know how close he'd come to winning that battle, but I had won, so was his master. I never abused him, and he never offered to buck again. How I wanted to take him with me, but it would be harder to stay inconspicuous with two horses.

I was about ready to leave, but just had to say goodby to Buck again. I was standing there with one hand on his neck, and the other rubbing his nose, when Emmanuel took the situation in his hands. He knew how much I thought of that Buck horse.

Finally he let out a breath and a long line of Spanish, only part of which I understood. He ended with, "Dammit Red, either you take Buck with you, or else I'm going to run yelling to the boss right now. Hell man, you know there isn't another man in the country that can ride and get along with that ornery "caballo cabron" anyway."

If I took him, I thought, I could pack several days' grain supply and a few more personal belongings.

"Emmanuel, you blackmailer, hurry and help me get a pack back on him, before I change my mind."

Buck, Blizzard, and I left together in the black of the night. I was glad it was dark, when Emmanuel and I parted. It was hard to keep the lump down.

Had I stayed at the ranch and seen the trouble through, many things would have turned out differently, but I don't know to this day, whether it would have been for better or worse.

It was a long night. I hashed over my problems, and might have returned to the ranch; but there seemed to be an impelling force driving me on. I couldn't turn back even once when I tried to.

I wasn't so concerned about being seen after leaving the ranch. I was in cow country, and there were quite a few cowboys drifting around from ranch to ranch. The few people I saw off in the distance during the next week's travel, never paid any attention to me.

I didn't know where I was going, but I sort of had an idea about Montana. There were several big chuckwagon ranches up in that country, and lots of remote line camps where a fellow could drop out of sight for six months at a time and never be seen or missed.

The season of the year was getting well into the fall; so I had to be careful to stay out of the real high country crossing Colorado. It seemed like a better idea to circle to the west of the high mountains rather than to the east. There were too many people, for one thing, along the eastern slope.

A couple weeks later, I was over in western Colorado, sticking high above the ranches, farms, and towns. The air felt like the weather was about to change, but when I made my camp that night, it was under a still, bright, beautiful star-studded sky.

I found a good sheltered spot under an overhanging shelf rock for my camp. I had a pretty good bedroll, with a tarp and several blankets. Of course, if it got real cold, I could use my saddle blanket for an extra cover. When you stay outside all the time, you get more accustomed to cool weather. Also, there was lots of good firewood handy.

Early the next morning, I woke up cold, and discovered there was a couple inches of snow on the ground, and more falling. It didn't look like such a good place to be then, way up on the side of the mountain.

The fire had burned out, but I had stacked up some dry kindling by the rocks, so it didn't take long to get a blaze going.

The horses were doing OK. They'd worked over under a large pine tree. If they'd had some hay, they would have been as comfortable as in a barn.

I still had a little grain as I'd been rationing it out to them. They were glad to get a larger helping that morning than usual.

Daylight was slow getting there after breakfast. It looked to me like we were in for an early winter; like maybe we'd better start working down to lower country. We were far enough away from New Mexico. Maybe we'd get by, if I just acted like I was drifting, and not on the dodge.

About noon that day, we were going down a narrow valley that appeared like it might empty into a larger valley up ahead a ways. The snow was getting deep and still falling gently, but the country was opening up and easier to travel through.

Directly we rounded a bend, and there ahead of us, the snow had quit falling. Coming in from our right was a larger valley full of cattle, drifting downhill.

It was a beautiful sight; that trail of good Hereford cattle; two, three, or more abreast, strung on down the valley a mile or more. It was quite awhile before the drags came by with a couple riders behind them.

They pulled up their horses and turned in my direction; so I rode down to them.

They greeted me with a friendly, "Howdy". I mentioned that I was just drifting through the country and had gotten caught in the snow; so decided I'd better get down to where traveling was a little easier.

They suggested I just as well tag along with them, as their trail was about the only way to get down out of the hills unless I was a bird.

They had a big fenced-in pasture and a camp at the foot of the mountain. Those cows knew where they were going. It didn't take much driving to get them out of the snow country.

There was a good horse corral and a stack of hay which my horses enjoyed that night.

The line camp was a good one. Being in the mountains, it was made from logs, and was a real cozy place to spend the night in.

After supper we sat and visited for awhile. It turned out that the two cowboys were father and son, and they owned the cows and the ranch. They had some winter range down on the breaks of the Colorado River, and were moving their cows down there. When they discovered I was just drifting around looking for a job, they offered me the winter camp job of looking after their cows.

It was a long way from town, and the road to it was almost impassable for anything except a team and wagon. They expected the man that took the job to stay out there all winter.

I hated to appear too eager, to let them know that was exactly what I was looking for; but finally after bantering back and forth over whether or not I wanted to be that far from town for all winter, I finally let them persuade me to give it a try.

They didn't ask my name, where I was from, or nothing. Just looked me and my outfit over, and decided I could handle the job OK.

That was just what I wanted; a place to drop out of sight for the next six months or so. I agreed to take the job, but only for the winter. In the spring, after the cows were gathered and headed back to higher country, I wanted to be free to go up to Montana.

The winter camp, which was more than thirty miles on down in the Colorado Breaks, wasn't much of a castle. It was pretty well built, though, out of rocks and adobe, and set in a good sheltered place out of the wind, where it got the benefit of all the sunshine possible.

There was close to a section fenced in for a horse and weak- cow pasture. A rocked-in spring ran out of the hill back of the camp, and the run-off ran through the horse lot before it soaked into the ground. There was a good little horse barn and a stack of hay that looked like it would last through the winter if I took care of it.

I had about 3000 cows to look after, on a strip of country some ten miles wide by twenty long. A lot of it was rough, with several side draws, but it was a good sheltered range.

There were a few windmills to be checked, and a few places I'd have to watch in case the weather turned off real cold and stayed that way quite awhile.

One of the main things was just to leave a set of fresh shod horse tracks around the country; so somebody wouldn't get the idea the cattle were left untended, and get ideas about driving off some of them.

Another thing was the coyotes and mountain lions some years got thick in that area. The rancher left me a 30-30 and a case of shells. I got quite a few hides that winter, and had almost the whole floor and inside walls carpeted with pelts by spring.

He also left me a couple "green broke" young horses. He figured with Buck and Blizzard, I'd have enough horseflesh to carry me all winter.

Those "green broke" ponies turned out to be a couple spoiled horses. The man who'd been in that winter camp before, had tried to break them, but hadn't succeeded. They gave me a few skinned knuckles, and one of them even bucked me off a couple times, but by spring, they were about half broke.

That one that thought he was so tough got a surprise one morning. I put my pack saddle on him and hung all sort of junk and sacks full of tincans on it; then snubbed him fairly close to Buck's saddle horn. Then I pulled the bridle off Buck and turned them loose together in the big corral.

Every time that young horse would spook and go into a bucking fit, big old Buck would make a lunge and go the other way. Down would come Mister Smart Bronco, with his head almost jerked off. It didn't take Buck long to teach that young fellow to be afraid to misbehave.

The boss would come out to my camp about once a month, bringing me a few groceries and some old magazines and newspapers. Once, after he'd been out, I was unwrapping a slab of bacon wrapped in newspaper in addition to the thin brown paper.

I was just casually looking through it, when an article caught my eye. It told about a wild brazen cowboy attacking four peaceful Spanish boys with a branding iron. It broke the neck of one of the boys and killed him, and hospitalized two of the others with serious injuries to their heads. He had attacked them only because they were Spanish. After beating them with the iron, he had managed to flee the town before he could be apprehended; but the officials expected to locate him as soon as one of the Spanish boys could talk. He was named Rodriguez, and seemed to know something or other about their attacker. He would talk and tell what he knew as soon as he was able, but he apparently had a broken jaw from being hit by the branding iron.

The story never mentioned anything about the four Mexes having long sharp knives, or about one of them slitting the skin of the cowboy's throat in a long enough gash to leave a scar for life.

I hated to be outlawed, but I never felt the least bit sorry for that "cabron". As far as I was concerned, he butted into someone else's business, and me hitting him with my fist so hard it broke his neck was no more than self defense.

They didn't know my name. As a matter of fact, nobody at the ranch in New Mexico actually knew my name. They had nicknamed me "Booger Red" that night after my battle with Buck, and that's all I was ever called, there. That was back in the days before social security and withholding statements. What wages I had drawn while there were all paid in cash.

If nobody recognized my two horses, the chances were no one would ever locate me. Anyhow, I didn't plan to lose any sleep over what had happened.

It's always been a thrill to me to ride and learn a new country.

I sure learned to like that Colorado River breaks country. It was really a good winter range. Most of the winter storms blowed over our heads and lodged up against the mountains.

There was one high place sort of in the center of the range, that I could see most of the country from. I made lots of rides up across that hill. Every time I rode up there, I'd stop and set awhile, and devour the scenery with my eyes.

Late one day, while I was idling away the afternoon up on that hill, I spotted a coyote out on the end of the ridge that ran quite a ways before dropping off towards the river. He was too far away to get a shot at; so I decided to see if I could ride down the ridge and get closer to him.

Mr. Coyote got wind of me and gave me the slip, before I reached him. I continued on up the ridge, thinking maybe I'd drop off towards the river and ride up it a ways before going back to camp.

I pulled up at the point of the ridge, to study the country a bit, before dropping off. There, down in the flat which had been out of my view since leaving the high point, was a man ahorseback. When he saw me, he turned and rode up to where I was.

He was a cowboy; there was no mistaking that. He was riding a good horse, and had a good-looking bridle and double rig saddle. He looked like he was on the drift, but he was doing it with just one horse. That doesn't let you carry much extra provisions or bedding.

His horse didn't look very ganted up, but that cowboy did. He looked like he hadn't had a good meal in quite awhile.

He was friendly though. He rode up to me with a smile, and the old Indian greeting sign of holding your right hand up, palm forward at shoulder height, and gave me the customary greeting of "How".

I returned his salute, and asked him, "How's things going for you?"

He answered they would be better, he guessed, if he had a smoke.

I carried the "makins" with me, Bull Durham and wheat-straw papers, so fished them out of my vest pocket and tossed them to him.

I was studying him while he built his smoke. He was about my age and size, and from what I could see, appeared to have reddish-brown hair.

When he finished rolling his smoke, he started to toss the makins back to me; but stopped when he saw that I'd fished another part of a sack out of another pocket, and also had a smoke about ready.

I looked across at him and told him to "Keep 'em. I got some more at camp."

We sat there enjoying our smokes without talking for awhile. Finally I asked him if he was traveling far.

"Yeah, I was heading for Arizona. In good shape, too, until the other night up in the junction. I got tangled up with some old gal that was a whole lot tougher than she looked. Before the night was over, she about cleaned me out."

I guess he felt he had to explain to me why he didn't have any makins with him.

His pack under his blanket roll looked pretty flat, like he might be out of a whole lot more than smokes.

I had lots of grub at camp, and it got pretty lonesome at times, living by myself all the time; but I didn't want to insult this cowboy by suggesting he might need a handout.

I sat there thinking of some of the times when I'd been on the drift and run low on grub. A well-stocked line camp sure looks good then.

"If you're not in a big hurry to get to Arizona, why don't you come on over to my camp. I got a corral and a good stack of hay and quite a bit of grub on hand."

We studied each other for a few minutes before he answered with, "That sounds like a winner. I guess my horse and I both could stand it."

I had a fresh venison hanging in my saddle room. After we took care of our horses, I carved off a large share of a hind quarter to take back to the cabin with me.

Biscuits and gravy, venison steak, fried spuds and pinto beans was what we ate that night. That cowboy must have put away five pounds of grub. He sure was starved. I was afraid he was going to make hisself sick he ate so much.

It was a good evening. We found we had much in common and really enjoyed visiting with each other.

This cowboy used the nickname of Sandy quite a bit in those days. The name fit him, but he told me that wasn't how he come to have the name. He'd got it up on the Antlers while riding out in the Shoulderblade country. He'd just gone to work for Tschurgy. The first day out, a big old Appy horse had bucked him off over in Sand Creek. The whole crew saw it. That big, stout old pony had blowed up just as they were crossing the creek bottom. He said the crew told him afterwards, there was so much sand kicked in the air, that it looked like a giant Jimmycane had swooped down in the creekbed and was really taking over.

He said, after that Appy piled him, and the air cleared up enough for the crew to come hunt for him, he was so covered with sand, they could hardly find him. He's packed that "Sandy" nickname ever since.

Sandy was the first cowboy of my own caliber I'd visited with since Emmanuel and I had parted company down in New Mexico.

Late that night, Sandy asked me if I drank any hard liquor.

"Not very often, but sometimes on special occasions. I don't have a drink in the camp though."

He told me he didn't use it very much either, but sometimes he did like a little snort on holidays.

"Is this a holiday?"

"You don't know what day it is?"

When I shook my head no, he got up and headed outside, saying he'd be back in a minute.

When he came back in, he had an unopened pint of "Old Cornfield,," straight grain whiskey.

He held out the bottle and said, "Red, I'd like to buy you a drink and wish you a "Merry Christmas." This is Christmas Eve."

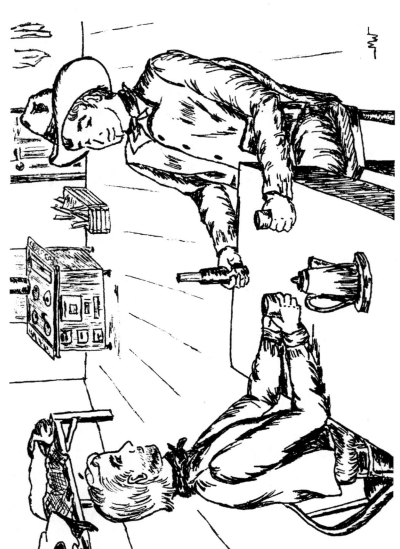

"Red, I'd like to buy you a drink and wish you a Merry Christmas. This is Christmas Eve."

We only spent one other Christmas Eve together after that one.

We watered down that little bottle of his, and sipped on it till way late in the night. It sure seemed good to have his company that night.

Sandy was all for leaving out on his journey to Arizona the next day, but I managed to talk him out of it. When I finally got desperate to keep him there for a while longer, I told him it wouldn't be very polite to leave on Christmas Day.

Alright, he agreed to stay until the next day. His "next day" extended until a couple days after New Year's.

We had a good week. Sandy rode with me every day, and we sure roped a lot of cows. Everything that remotely looked like it needed doctoring, got roped. We did get several in-grown horns cut off, and all the bad eyes fixed up, that we could find.

In that week I learned why Sandy was in a hurry to get south. He had a winter job down at Castle Hot Springs, wrangling dudes. It didn't pay much, but a fellow got to chouse the good-looking gals quite a bit. The season had already started, and he should have been there by Christmas. However, they knew him and expected him to show up; so he was sure the job would still be his when he got there.

This past summer he'd driven a sightseeing stagecoach for the Park Service up in Yellowstone, and he planned to return to it again the next year.

That gave me an opening to tell him about my six horse hitch experience, and how much I liked doing it. When he heard that, he got all excited and said he was going to come back by my camp and take me up to the Jackson Hole country with him the next spring.

That night after supper, Sandy got real serious, and told me he was going to leave the next day. He didn't want me to say a thing to try to stop him. He would like to stay there all winter, but he just had to leave.

I sat silent thinking for awhile before saying, "OK, I won't say no more, if you"ll tell me something straight."

He looked at me questioningly before saying, "What's that?"

"How much money you got on you?"

"Not much, " he said, "but enough to make it."

I studied him awhile; then got up and went over to my bed. I fished out an old billfold, and took out the contents, six ten-dollar bills.

I shuffled them out in two even piles, and pushed one of them to Sandy.

"No, Red," were his remorseful words. "I've already sponged enough off you. I'll not take it."

"Sandy," I said, getting real serious. "You'll take that and all the grub you can pack or I'll fight you till I outwind you; then stuff this money in your pocket and load you on your horse and send you on your way. So, if you want to show your respect and save us both a whale of a beating; you'll take it as a loan, and get on your way. Then you can get back by next spring and take me up north with you."

He sat and thought several things over for quite awhile, and started to say something several times. Then he'd stop and do some more thinking.

Finally he let his breath out and said, "OK, Red, if that's the way you want it. It's a loan and I'll pay you back some way some day."

It was a long long time before we settled accounts, but the last time I saw him we had a last smoke together; and all accounts were squared away between us.

When he left the next morning, I wondered if we'd ever meet again. Life is so uncertain.

That was a lonesome day out there on the Colorado river breaks.

Then the weather turned off bad, with a norther dumping way more snow on that range than was customary. We'd have been in real bad shape, had the wind not come up the next day, and blowed most of it off part of the grass. The way it wound up, in a few days, was with lots of deep drifts and a few bare spots. We had four sheds full of cottonseed meal scattered over the range for just such emergencies.

I had to make a circle each day, putting out a few sacks of feed at each place; all the while looking for weak cattle or ones that was drifted in, and get them out to feed. I spent a week fighting that snowy range each day, putting in about sixteen hours a day. I never had time to think about Sandy or that sunny Arizona range.

About a week later, a chinook blowed in, and for a few days it was mud everywhere.

One evening as I rode up to camp, I see smoke coming out of the chimney. It was about three weeks since Sandy had left. I hadn't seen anyone from the ranch headquarters since shortly after Thanksgiving. I'd begun to wonder if they had forgotten about me.

I spotted the boss's horse and pack horse in my corral, before I got up to camp, where he met me.

"Howdy, cowboy. Chuck'll be ready by the time you take care of your horse, and get your muddy hands and face washed."

"Howdy yourself, Boss. I'll be right there. It'll be a real treat to have a house-maid cooked meal."

We had lots of talking to do that night. How the cattle were holding up; where the grass was still good; and how low we were getting on cakes in the caches. The boss said he'd have a couple wagon loads of cake brought out as soon as the mud dried enough to hold a wagon up.

"You know," he said, "If you can handle eight head of horses on a big freight wagon, you could come back to headquarters with me, spend a night in town, and then drive one of the outfits back out here."

For some reason, I detected a hidden question in his words. I used the excuse to check the fire in the cookstove and pour us a refill of coffee before answering him.

"Well, I'd sure enjoy some headquarters company and the city lights for a night. I wouldn't mind helping load the cake, but I don't believe I'd be much help with a big freight hitch like that. I've helped hook up the chuckwagon mules a good many times, but that's about all I know about it."

The boss stayed for a few days and rode with me, looking over the cows and range. He was pretty observative. He told me on the second day, that he'd counted six or eight head of cows that I'd cut the ingrown horns off of, and it looked like I must have doctored a good many bad eyes.

He was real pleased because it looked like I had stayed busy riding. He hadn't seen anything that I hadn't taken care of.

The day he left to go back to headquarters, we talked again about me going back with him for a few days. I begged off by telling him how much I'd like to go, but I had my extra saddle horses to look after. I also had a few weak cows that had little calves, that were in the wrangle pasture. I took cake to them regularly; so maybe I'd better stay there at camp.

"If I went to town, I might get to liking it and not want to come back out here. Besides, I wouldn't be much help with the freight hitches anyhow."

The boss acted kind of relieved. Presently, he told me that he'd been down in New Mexico visiting some relatives. One of the stories they'd got a kick out of telling, was about a red-headed cowboy who had tackled a whole bunch of knife-wielding Mexes and had cleaned out the bunch of them. The squabble had started over the Mexes spooking a freight team the cowboy had been driving, and causing a runaway. It must have been quite a sight.

"The runaway?" I asked.

"No, the fight in the saloon that night. I guess that cowboy must have really tore things up."

I was glad that scar on the side of my neck was hidden by my neckscarf. I could imagine I felt it tingling.

"I reckon some fellas get quite a kick out of that barroom brawling. I never cared much for it myself."

The rest of the winter passed without much excitement. The cake was shipped out a week or so later. I would sure like to have gotten hold of those ribbons on one of those big wagons. I could have shown that boy how to shape up that big hitch in a hurry and really got some work out of them. It was all I could do, to let on like I didn't know how to drive.

February and March passed by slowly. I rode almost every day, and kept busy, which helped.

One day in April, I noticed that I had been looking to the southwest skyline quite a bit. That was when I realized I was waiting and hoping Sandy would soon show up. It was going to be very disappointing if he didn't.

April soon was almost gone. I'd been drifting the cattle up out of the low flat country; so a gather in the middle of May would be easier. Then it would be time to head to the high country with the herd.

I rode up on a little bunch of cows. One big, stout old wild bossy had a hind leg stuck in an old rusty bucket. That was all the excuse I needed, to jerk my lass rope down and take out after her. I rode right in on her, throwed a good loop right around her horns, jerked my slack; then dropped the slack down around her hind end, and then rode on by.

I busted her hard, and figured I could get the can off her hind leg and get her turned loose before she aroused; but I was a trifle slow. When I jerked my rope off her, she flipped me off her shoulder, lit on her feet, and was sure on the hook. She took to snorting right in my hip pocket.

I'd been riding one of my broncs that day, and had my reins tied to my lass rope. That didn't keep him from spooking and trying to get away, while I was trying to get to him and away from that cow.

I was in trouble. It looked to me like I was going to have to let go of my horse, so I could turn around and fight old Sookey to keep her from running over me.

About that time I heard what I took to be a horse running towards me from the southwest. At the same time a most welcome voice yelling, "Stay with it cowboy! Stay with it, Red!" Then a mounted cowboy shot between me and that cow that almost had a horn in my hip pocket.

It took awhile to get my bronco quieted down enough so I could get up to him. Then I turned to make sure who had come to my rescue. Sandy had a grin a mile long as he rode back toward me, coiling up his rope. Old Sookey was hightailing for the bunch; she'd had enough of cowboys for awhile.

"Sandy, you dude chaser! It's sure good to see you." I panted, as I hauled the makins out of my shirt pocket and tossed them to him.

We had lots of visiting to catch up on. I kept Sandy talking till way late in the night, telling about all that had happened to him and the dude gals down in Arizona all winter.

Sandy stayed and rode with me the rest of the spring. When May 15th rolled around, it was time to head the herd for the high country. We had everything under control. By the 20th, we had all the cows kicked through the boundary fence gate, and had the lower country cleaned.

It was time for me to draw my wages and head for the Jackson Hole country with Sandy.

Chapter III

YELLOWSTONE STAGECOACHES

I guess we were quite a sight to them, with our big sombreros, silk neck scarves, and buckskin vests.

The day we rode into the ranch up there in Wyoming is one I'll remember all my life. The ranch had opened up early that year to accommodate a large group from back east. Sandy hadn't known of these plans the fall before, and the ranch boss had no way to get ahold of him to let him know of the change.

There was a whole crowd of interested spectators there in the yard watching our approach. I guess we were quite a sight to them, with our big sombreros, silk neck scarves, and buckskin vests. Sandy wore a pair of batwing chaps, and I had on "woolies". Sandy had on a pair of five point five inch Mexican Chihuahua spurs. I used those big 21 point rowel, silver mounted Crocketts. We both wore our six-shooters. Since the boss in Colorado had given me the 30-30 that I'd used all winter, I had it hanging on my riggin' also.

I was trailing Buck with our packs on him. I guess we were as interesting a sight to them as they were to me. This was the first time I was ever around a dude ranch. Since Sandy had filled me full of stories about all the goodlooking dude gals that would be there, I was really looking over the prospects out of the corners of my eyes.

Sandy rode up to the crowd ahead of me. He steps off his horse and shakes hands with a distinguished looking westerner standing there with the crowd.

"Howdy, Boss," he says. "What'd you do, jump the gun and open up early this year, or are we late?"

"Howdy yourself, you drifting cowboy. It's good to see you, and you're just in time. We opened early for a special group this year."

"Boss, I'd like for you to meet a friend of mine. He's shore enough a cowboy, I can vouch for that. He's looking for a job, and says he can skin the hide right off of a six horse hitch. I'll bet he can too; but if you got a job for him, you'll have to be your own judge of what he can do."

Turning to me, he says, "Come on, Red, get off your horse and shake hands with the boss."

I didn't know Sandy was so full of wind. If it hadn't been for one bee-yootiful raven-haired girl standing there in the group, smiling at me, I think I might have spooked and stampeded right away from there.

By the time I got off my horse, the boss was introducing Sandy to the group there. I stepped up just as the introductions got around to the black haired gal, and this is what took place.

The boss was saying, "and this little beauty, my friend, is off limits to you. She come down from Dillon to help us out this year. Sandy, this is Monte."

Sandy was really knocked for a loop. I think he fell in love with her right then and there, as he took off his big sombrero with his left hand and shook hands with Monte with his right hand, just like you do when meeting a man. I was completely forgotten as everybody watched Sandy and Monte, and listened to the words exchanged between them.

Sandy talked with his eyes and actions, but Monte came out with words.

"It's pleased I am to meet you cowboy, but cowboys aren't new to me. I've already been warned about how you fall in love with a new girl each week; so if you"ll give my hand back to me, and introduce your hairy-legged friend to us, we'll get along fine."

Everybody got a good laugh out of Monte's referring to my wooly chaps as the "hairy-legged friend."

Sandy finally came to, and presented me to his boss and the others there; but I did notice he tried to stay between me and Monte. I think he was already getting jealous.

After the introductions, the boss says to me, "So you're a six horse hitch skinner are you?"

"I've handled them some," I admitted.

Whereupon the boss turned to Sandy and says, "We were just trying to figure out something exciting to do to entertain the group with, this afternoon. If Red wants to try out for the job, that wild hitch that Tex drove last year is out in the corral. You guys can go hitch them up and hook them to the heavy Yellowstone coach and work them in the ring. If things go alright, maybe we'll all go for a ride afterwards."

Everybody looked towards me, and Sandy asks, "What do you say, Red?"

"That's what we came up here for. Let's get with it."

That was a good hitch. All tall, rangy horses, sixteen to seventeen hands, and solid colored bays.

I asked Sandy to tell me what he knew about those horses. They'd been worked two or three years and were a good responsive bunch of horses, but were pretty fiery. They might run off if they had the chance.

The leaders were Charlie and Jake. None of them had been worked since the fall before. They were pretty skittish when we were harnessing them; so I took each team out in the lot and drove them in a circle at a trot and gallop for a few minutes to warm them up before hooking the six together on that Yellowstone coach.

They were a couple hands full when we hooked up; and they wanted to run off. There was a good large working ring there to warm them up in. As soon as I had them under control, I let them out to a gallop. We circled that arena hard until they were ready to slow down of their own accord. They really were a good hitch. As soon as the horses figured out I could handle them, they became very responsive and really worked a figure 8 pattern smoothly.

I stopped and started them out again several times in the hour or so I was working there in the arena. Then I drove over to the gate and told the boss that if he was satisfied, I was ready to go for a spin out in the open. Sandy had been on his saddle horse while we were working in the arena. He said he'd go along outside for the ride in case we needed him.

The group was ready and willing, so we loaded that old Yellowstone coach down and headed out.

We had a good ride that afternoon, and when we got back to the ranch, the boss said, "Red, the job's yours, and we're glad to have you with us." I stayed there two seasons and drove that six horse hitch for them, before finally drifting on again.

The regular season was due to open in about a week; so Sandy and I were kept pretty busy, getting up his horses, getting everything shod, and warmed up to the harness.

Monte was true to her word. She knew cowboys. They weren't an interesting novelty to her, but they were her kind of men.

She was always friendly to me. We had many interesting times together, but I never could get any closer to her than being a cherished friend. Sandy used to get so jealous of me, for no reason I tried to tell him. He couldn't believe that I wasn't part of the reason that he and Monte had so many quarrels. He just couldn't see that he was trying to rush her too much.

Monte loved him so much, and she'd talk to me about it; but I couldn't help either one of them. I was in love with her too. I enjoyed talking with her and taking her for a ride on my coach, but I never touched her or held her, or told her how beautiful she was. I knew that some day, she and Sandy would quit quarreling, and things would take care of themselves in due order.

Driving that stagecoach in Wyoming was about the most interesting thing that happened to me in my life. I enjoyed driving that six horse hitch there more than anything else I've ever done.

Sandy was a good driver, but he seemed to have to work at it. Driving was natural for me. My hands and fingers would just seem to almost work the lines by theirselves. It used to bother Sandy somehow.

One event that became very popular with the guests there, was one Sandy figured out to try to prove he was a more skilled driver than I was. He designed an obstacle course in the big arena. Every day he would take his coach in and work the course for a half hour or so. This had been going on for a couple weeks. One Saturday noon at the dinner table, in front of a whole house full of guests, Sandy announced to the group without consulting me beforehand, that he and I were going to put on a driving exhibition and contest in the arena that afternoon with the coaches. He invited the whole group of guests and all the crew down to watch.

Everybody likes to see a good contest, it seems. At least I think everybody on the ranch was there in the bleachers to see the exhibition that afternoon.

The arena was a large one. Somehow Sandy already had the pattern stakes set up when we got there. He had the boss and another fellow with stop watches at the entry gate. The idea was for them to start their watches when a coach entered, and to stop when each coach rumbled out past them.

The course was marked out to a large circle, going into a figure 8, then a sharp U turn, and exit from the arena. There would be a five second penalty charged for each stake knocked down, if any were.

Sandy said he'd drive the pattern slow; then I could go in and drive it once slow to try it out. Then he would take the first time trial. The total distance through the course measured over 3,000 feet.

Sandy entered at a gallop, and had the crowd on their feet cheering him. He was always so much fuller of bright conversation with the guests than I was, that I guess they all felt they knew him better than they did me. Anyway, they were rooting for him as their hero.

He ran a good course, coming pretty close to two or three stakes, which brought responses from the crowd each time, but he never touched one. When he came charging out through the gate, it was to the accompaniment of loud cheers from the crowd.

The boss and the other stop watch man checked with each other. They discovered they had both clocked it exactly two minutes. That figures out at over 20 miles an hour, which isn't bad time for circling and doing figure 8's.

I knew Monte and Sandy had been quarreling the night before, but it surprised me when she came by and asked if she could ride in the coach in the contest with me.

I wanted to tell her "No", but when she puckered up her lips and mouthed the word, "Please," without saying it, my restraint melted. Looking away, I said, "It's your neck you're risking," but that's what she wanted. I never could refuse her anything.

I was sure I could beat Sandy, so as I came around in front of the grandstand, I slammed the brake on hard and hauled in on the lines with all my might. As the coach skidded to a stop, I reached up and tipped my hat to the crowd without taking the lines out of that hand. I squalled at the horses and was again instantly in a dead run.

I got a little careless when I made the U turn. I took it hard enough to sling the rear end of the coach around in a broad skid, and it smacked one of the stakes and sent it flying across the arena. We came out through that gate in a high lope and Monte hanging on with both hands.

When the boss compared his stopwatch with the other one, they discovered I'd run the course in 1:55 seconds. That was five seconds faster than Sandy's time, but since I'd clipped one stake and had to take a five second penalty, that made it a draw.

Sandy wanted to rerun, and run the tie off right then; but I refused, saying my horses were too charged up; that I would be willing to run it over the next week.

I guess we rerun that race and course fifteen times in those two years. Sandy only beat me twice in all those races. The second time he beat me was the last race we ran. Monte was riding with him that time. By then, they had quit their quarreling, and were planning to be married that very evening.

Sandy ran the course in 1:50 seconds that day and never touched a stake.

I got too wild and wiped out a whole row of stakes. I lost that race and the girl that day, but the experience from those stagecoach races opened up a whole new life for me later on.

Sandy and Monte were married that night, there at the ranch.

Since it was the end of the guest season and had been a pretty busy summer, we all really unwound that night and had one whale of a party. We had a local band come in, and had a dance in the big barn for the whole community. I don't think there were very many people who got to sleep before daylight the next morning.

The next day, the last of the summer guests left. All the help was packing and getting ready to pull out, but everybody was waiting for Sandy and Monte to leave on their honeymoon. They had an almost new Ford car which they had recently purchased.

Since Sandy and I were pals, and I had been the best man at their wedding, I'd agreed to get their car up and have it all ready for their getaway that afternoon. I sure did have it ready too.

With the help of the other kids there, we lettered and ribboned it all up, and had several strings of tin cans and old shoes tied to the back end of it. Unknown to everyone there, I had located some special fireworks that would go off after I had driven the car up to the getaway departure spot. When I flipped a hidden switch, it would set them off when the auto was next started.

It was a blast!

Sandy and Monte finally came running out of their cabin through all our cheers and well wishes. They piled into their new Ford, and hit the starter. Since I'd had it running not long before, it took right off. Those fireworks took a few seconds to get into the action, but when they did, it was spectacular!

First, there was a loud whistling sound, like all the tires were losing air at the same time. The Ford was moving ahead at a good start by the time the whistling ended, when a series of loud explosions went off, and a cloud of blue smoke engulfed the whole area. A few more booms ended the fireworks, but by this time, Sandy and Monte were sure their Ford had completely blowed to pieces. They stopped, and were hurriedly trying to get out and away from it before it completely disintegrated.

The crowd went wild, as I very innocently went out to aid Monte and Sandy. After the excitement died down, I had an awful hard time convincing them that nothing serious had happened to their car; that it would be safe to re-enter it and continue on their trip. Everyone thought it was a whale of a Chevaree trick.

It sure was lonesome around that ranch that night after they were gone. I'd promised the boss, though, that I'd stick it out a few days, to get the shoes pulled off the horses and get the equipment put away for the winter. I'd also agreed to trail the horses out to their winter pasture before I left. I had lots of time to think and remember, while finishing up those chores.

I'd found a heavy gold engineer's pocket watch in a pawn shop, which I bought and had Sandy's name engraved on it, and gave to him for a wedding present. He was as pleased as if it had been a million dollars.

Some people might think it strange the present I gave Monte that night, but it was what she wanted I'm sure, and she still has it.

That first day there on the ranch, Monte fell in love with my old outlaw horse, Buck. How she used to pester me to let her ride him, but I wouldn't let her get on him. Sandy had taken a seat on Buck a good many times, and never was able to stick him out. He sure was a one man horse, or so I thought. Until one day coming in with the stagecoach, I spied somebody loping down the road on a very familiar looking buckskin horse. I almost swallowed my chew of tobacco.

Monte was grinning as proud as could be. I wanted to get mad at her, but just couldn't. She said she'd been riding Buck every chance she could get when I was away from the ranch.

I just gave up protesting and told her to go ahead and ride him whenever she wanted.

That night of the wedding, I gave Monte a bill of sale to my old Buck horse. I knew he would be happy.

When I headed south that fall, it was just me and Blizzard that drifted out across Idaho and on down through Utah, and over into

Arizona. That's a beautiful ride down across there in the fall, if you stay close to the mountains, but it sure was lonesome traveling by myself that time.

I heard there were some big cow outfits that ran chuckwagons over in the Saligman country; so I headed that way.

Money and jobs were pretty scarce, but I got on as an extra hand with the fall roundup wagon.

I pulled my share of the load and worked hard, but kept pretty much to myself. I didn't buddy up with any of the crew. I didn't want any friends and didn't care to go to town. When the fall roundup work was done, about Christmas time, all the extra hands were let go.

It didn't amount to much, but I'd saved part of my summer's wages and most of the fall's earnings; so I decided to drift on south and spend the winter in old Mexico; maybe do a little prospecting on the way.

I found a few traces of color that winter, but never made enough money to pay for very much grub. I worked my way clear down into old Mexico, and accidentally stumbled onto one of the best put together ranches I've seen in a long time.

They had winter range and summer range, spring and fall country; all in a circular area around the headquarters, which lay in a beautiful valley. It was full of running water, with alfalfa fields, orchards and gardens. The buildings were all made of adobe, stuccoed on the outside. With their red tile roofs, it sure was a picturesque sight.

That ranch was a beauty, and I might have stayed there a long time, but for one thing. There were too many flashing brown eyes and lovely Mexican maidens; but I am getting ahead of my story.

As I rode up to the ranch, a group of vaqueros were corralling a good sized herd of cows into a large lot, fixing to brand calves. Those vaqueros were having some kind of a problem putting the cattle through the gate. While I was out a ways, about fifty head of calves and a few cows ducked out between the cowboys and were about to make their getaway, as all the Mexicans were needed right then to plug the hole and hold the other cows to keep the whole herd from getting away.

The cattle that broke out were headed right toward me, where I was sitting on Blizzard. I was able to turn them and curve them back into the side of the corral fence, just a short ways from where the crew was fastly getting the main herd back under control. I had my hands full, holding the escaped herd there until a couple of the vaqueros were able to leave their positions at the gate and come to my rescue.

We finally got all the cattle corralled; then the boss came over and thanked me for giving them a hand. He told me they were having a little branding party, and that if I would like to stay and join the branding, they would have a big feed and a regular fiesta that evening.

Those vaqueros were all so friendly, I immediately felt quite welcome, and I certainly enjoyed the festivities that night.

I got along good with all the Mexicans there, and stayed through the spring roundup and several more fiestas. If I hadn't been so doggone girl-shy, I probably would have stayed down there a long long time, but there was a sixteen year old girl named Lolita, and she got such a crush on me I had to leave.

Now you know why I sometimes sing that old Mexican song softly to myself—

"Spanish is the loving tongue,
Soft as Music, light as spray,
'Twas a girl I learned it from,
Living down Sonora way."

Chapter IV

THE RESCUE

In the winter when I was drifting down through Arizona, I'd come across a reward poster that had aroused me at the time. It had been on my mind much of the time during the spring round up.

This poster was different from most posters as it was for some horses that presumably had broken out of a pasture and had escaped to run wild on the desert. There were six of them, all geldings, and all four years old when they got away. That would make them five or six about this time. They were described as being fifteen hands, 1100 pounds; two buckskins, two grullas, and two dark bays. There was a $200.00 reward for their capture and return to the 2 Bar Ranch Headquarters.

The reward amounted to several month's wages at that time, but that wasn't what really excited me. I just wanted to go into that wild country, and try my hand at finding and capturing them.

It wasn't any problem locating the 2 Bar Ranch. In those days, it was a big outfit and ran lots of cattle. They kept a good crew of both Mexican and American cowboys, and they rode the best horses of anywhere. I decided I should ride out to their headquarters to talk to someone and see if the horses were still strayed, and if the reward was still out on them.

Almost everybody on the ranch was off on a cattle drive, or off the other way working on a movie that was being filmed on the ranch.

I was in luck that day though, as I found an old choreman and stopped to spend the time of day with him. I told him what I had in mind, and asked him if he might tell me any of the details; which way they figured those horses might have headed, and if the reward was still out, or anything more he could tell about them.

That old man was a wealth of information. He became quite talkative when he noticed I was riding a "Hamley" saddle, and his interest in me perked up.

He had been a bronc rider, and finally worked up to wagon boss on the "P" ranch out in the French Glen country in eastern Oregon. That Hamley saddle shore took him back to Oregon. He loved the country, but finally got too old to stand the hard winters anymore.

He gave me lots of ideas on where the strayed horses might be. Then he spent an hour telling me about the ranch, and all the Hollywood people staying there while they were making the movie.

After awhile, we got around to discussing the ranch's cowboy crew. I thought there might be some cowboys working there I'd known or worked with somewhere. The old choreman said they had lots of vaqueros on the ranch, but not many cowboys. For some reason that he didn't know, the big boss seemed to prefer the Mexican vaqueros over the cowboys. Even the wagon boss was a Mexican. He didn't know a great deal about him, as he hadn't been there for a long time, but he was mean to his horses and was always chasing some woman or other.

He did warn me I'd probably have better luck if I stayed out of the way of the wagon boss, but the reward was still out on the strayed broncs as far as he knew.

I took out on the trail of those broncs that afternoon, before any of the ranch crew returned.

The trail was pretty cold. It had been close to two years since the horses had gotten away. I spent a couple weeks roaming the high, wild country, hunting for horse sign, and checking out likely areas where they might be.

I jumped several small bands of wild horses, but none of them had any of the broncs with them that I was hunting.

74

I decided I needed to work back down closer to the headquarters, and take a little different look at the country. Then to try thinking like a bronco that had just escaped from a fenced-in pasture, and try to figure out which way they might have run.

While riding the country like this, a cowboy doesn't just sit his horse; he notices everything pertaining to the range and his work, and he keeps his hand in practicing to keep good at his work. One of my methods was like this: when I spotted a cow with a good sized unbranded calf, if I could read the cow's earmark plain, then I'd catch the calf for the practice and earmark it like it's mother was.

I finally got in trouble over doing it. I had worked back down within a few miles of the headquarters, and had high-pointed and scouted the country out real good. I hadn't seen a sign of a human, as far as I could see.

There was a good big open valley out ahead of me, with several side draws leading out of it. One of them sure looked like it was the type of country that I'd choose if I were a bronc. That was the direction I rode.

Riding up the side draw quite a ways, I came around a corner, right into a grassy opening. I ran smack into an old mossy horned cow with a great big slick-eared calf.

Three things happened all at once. The cow and calf broke and ran for the shelter of some close brush. Blizzard, being the good cowhorse that he was, immediately built right after them; and at the same time, I jerked down my lass rope and poked a loop in it. I made one swing, throwing quick to get it around that big calf's neck, before he reached the cover of the brush. His mammy vamoosed; but Blizzard and I had that fighting, bawling, scared hunk of calf, fair and square.

I'd got a good look at the cow's ears when we'd first run head on. She had a swallow fork in the right ear, and an underbit in the left; so I decided I just as well mark that calf before I turned him loose.

I'd just finished earmarking him, and straightened up to put my knife back in my pocket, when I heard a sound. Glancing up, I was confronted by two vaqueros with rifles pointing right at my chest.

75

I had my old 45 buckled on my hip, but never even thought about using it; but they didn't know that.

The first I knew, one of them was saying, "Stand up easy, with your hands in the air."

I'd tied the calf's legs together with my piggin' string before I'd earmarked him. He was still tied; so he had no choice but to lay there. Luckily for me, he didn't get away.

My attention was given a jolt with the next words of the Mex who was closest to me. Turning to the other fellow who was somewhat off to my left, he said, "Well, Rod, it sure looks like we've finally caught us a cow rustler."

When "Rod" answered, "Yeah, we could sure string him up, if there was any trees around big enough for it."

I was startled into glancing directly at him. I had heard that voice before, and that name!

That "Rod" was the same one who had been driving the car that had caused my runaway almost three years ago; and he was the one telling the story that night I'd whipped the bunch of them down in New Mexico and broken one's neck.

The night of that fight, I was clean shaven and dressed up. Luckily for me, this day, I had a heavy range beard and old torn, soiled working clothes. He never recognized me.

I had to speak up to try to convince them I wasn't stealing a calf; instead I was helping them out because I had put the ranch's earmark on it.

They admitted they could read the earmark, but insisted I had seen them following me, and that I had only put their mark on it to throw them off my track.

I wasn't getting anywhere with my defense, when another group of riders filed into the clearing where we were. Some of them were what I took to be part of the movie crew. They definitely included a couple women, and that many men who weren't cowboys or vaqueros.

Rod could see he couldn't discipline me like he wanted, but he could show off in front of the group, and he did; by dressing me down and ordering me off 2 Bar range.

Then he rode right up to me, but he made sure he didn't get between me and the rifle that was still pointed at my chest. I didn't know what he intended to do, but I am sure he was trying to get me to break or make a sudden move; so his rifleman could shoot me and claim I'd reached for my gun.

Suddenly, he leaned out of his saddle and slashed his quirt down across my shoulders and back.

Spurring his horse, he galloped off to his group, while his gunman backed his horse away from me until he figured he was out of range of my .45. Then he whirled his horse and galloped off after the others.

In a flash, I had my old 45 out and could have blasted him out of his riggin', but at the last instant, I got control of myself, and mastered the passionate desire to kill him. I just stood and watched Rod and his crew gallop around the corner and out of sight.

Finally, I turned the calf loose, and walked over to Blizzard. I had a right smart feeling welt across my shoulders, and could sure feel it burn as I raised my arm to grasp the horn to mount. Damn that Mexican! Someday, he and I were going to settle accounts.

And he was the wagon boss of the 2 Bar, and had just ordered me off the range. Damn again! That sure put a cloud over my horse hunting. Well, I wasn't going to let him scare me out yet. I didn't know exactly what I was going to do; but it looked like my plans to find that bunch of horses and collect the reward, were about ended. It'd probably be just as well to leave that part of Arizona and head farther west. Maybe I could find some kind of a riding job over California way.

I'd probably ridden ten or fifteen miles when I decided to climb up out of the valley to the higher country, to get a little better bearing. It was getting time to start hunting for some wild game; a bird or rabbit to shoot for supper, and look for a place to camp for the night.

I was just topping out over a ridge when suddenly I heard a rumbling sound, like horses running hard. I stopped, sitting still, straining my ears to pick up the direction the drumming was coming from. As sounds will do in the gentle desert breeze, it came and then faded out; then came again, louder. This time, there was another sound with the horses' hooves; one that I'd learned to know well. Real well. Up in the park in Wyoming. Horses running with a stagecoach. Sometimes it had been for fun; sometimes it had been bad. Today my heart jumped into high gear. This running, jingling, swishing sound sure had disaster in it."

Before Monte could continue her reading of the journal, I interrupted her to say, **"Annabelle, the second time I ever saw your mother, the sight almost scared me to death. That was many years ago, but that frightening, magnificent sight is still before my eyes, as if it had just happened. It is something I shall never forget. Now Monte, go ahead."**

Turning a page, Monte started in where she had left off.

"I topped that ridge in a good stiff gallop. The first thing I saw was Nanette. There she was, hanging out the side window of a runaway stagecoach, with six head of horses running as hard as they could go, and not a driver in sight. Nothing but that beautiful red hair of hers waving in the breeze. She wasn't screaming or crying; she was half way out of the window, trying to climb up onto the driver's box so she could try to get that hitch back under control!

In full pursuit, but far behind her, was a string of riders and a bunch of old Ford cars. I could see at a glance they were too far back to be of much help.

From where I was, I could see it wasn't over a quarter mile to the edge of the flat, where the road broke over the hill. There were too many big rocks along the road for a person to be able to jump out of the stage without being bashed to pieces.

It was plain something had to be done, and darn fast; otherwise that stage would be careening over that hill, and to what kind of downgrade I didn't know, but it was sure apt to be bad. In less time that in takes to tell about it, I was in action; spurring old Blizzard to full stride and then some, and jerking my rope down and building a loop. The only chance for rescue that I could see was to rope the far lead horse, and to set up as quick as I could. If I could pile up the leaders, maybe I could get the coach stopped before it reached the edge of the cliff.

It was a long time later before I ever found out what had caused that wild runaway. Maybe I better tell it now. The movie company was filming a western stagecoach picture. They were planning on the stage crossing the high plateau area and being attacked by hostile Indians. There was to be a chase across the flats; then a dash over the ridge, with a wild run down this crooked switchback road, and a final run onto the stage relay station. The movie company was planning on unloading the passengers just over the brink of the hill; then making the run down the grade as carefully as possible, with just the driver aboard and some "dummy" passengers inside. Everything was all set back there on the flat. Two hostlers were standing by the coach horses, the driver was on the box getting settled and pulling the lines up even, and the shotgun guard had started to climb up on the left side. Nanette, the first of the passengers, had just stepped into the coach, when somebody dropped a sixgun, and it discharged. It was a blank, of course, but the noise was just as loud.

Afterwards, everyone said that this hitch was supposed to be gun-shy proof, if there ever was one; but that was up to now. When that shell exploded right beside them, all six horses bolted in the wink of an eye.

As often happens, the hostlers had stood there so many times with nothing going wrong, that they figured there wasn't any need to hold on to the horses. If anything should go wrong, they were close enough to grab ahold. It was too late by then. Before they could bat an eye, the horses were all out of reach and going at a full gallop.

Ordinarily the driver couldn't have been thrown off either, but he said later, he'd just raised up and turned to fix the seat cushion. He had all six lines in one hand. When the horses bolted, it spun him around, and the side of the seat caught him under the knees. He was flipped over backwards and out into space before he knew what had happened. I'd have to give him lots of credit though. They said he pulled all the hide off his left hand flopping on the side of the coach trying to hang onto the lines.

79

As I felt him tumbling under me, I pulled my knees up under me and tried to go with the tumble, rolling as far out of his way as possible

The shotgun rider did a backflip clear out into the sagebrush. There wasn't a mounted man ready or close enough to catch the coach.

Nanette was slammed into the back seat and floor. By the time she could get her bearings and get straightened up, the horses were plumb spooked, and running like a cyclone was after them.

That's the way things were when I rode up on the scene.

I was only about 150 yards away when I first saw the stampede. This old cayuse of mine was fairly flying, giving me everything he had. We were really closing the gap, and I felt sure we'd make it. Then I just swallered my heart. As I closed in, I got a glimpse of the ground immediately ahead. Between me and the leaders, there wasn't an ounce of dirt; nothing but rocks and boulders. I was almost near enough to swing my loop, with just one more real bad spot ahead, when I felt Blizzard go crooked in the front end. I just had time to see one front foot swing crazily off to the side all busted to pieces, and feel him doing his best to keep upright and still pack me over the rocks. I jerked my toes out of my stirrups when I first felt him wobble. As I felt him tumbling under me, I pulled my knees up under me and tried to go with the tumble, rolling as far out of his way as possible.

We had been traveling at full speed. As he fell forward, I was catapulted over the last barrier of rocks.

Once in a hundred times, a man will land on his feet when a horse falls, and be able to stay upright. I surely would have fallen this time, but I just didn't have the chance. I was slammed smack into the right side of the wheel horse, just right to grab two hands full of hames. Since we were traveling about the same speed, I was able to hang on. It took a couple running strides for me to get my balance and size up the situation. Then I hit the ground with my feet and vaulted to the back of the wheel horse. I didn't know if he was broke to ride or not; anyway we were running too fast for him to buck. I could see the crest of the hill approaching fast, and I didn't have any time to stay on his back. As luck would have it, all six lines were together, between the wheel horses, on top of the tongue, and running back over the doubletrees and under the coach. I could see the only chance was to scoop up those lines, get into the driver's seat somehow, get my foot on the brake, and go to driving like I'd never driven before.

It's hard to climb into the driver's box from the tongue of a coach when it's standing still. Well, you ought to try it at a full stampede, bouncing over the rocks. I didn't know how I made it, but I did.

There wasn't much time to get the lines straightened out and in the right fingers. All I could do was grab them and pull hard with both fists, and slam my foot on the brake lever. I knew the way the horses had the bits and were running that I wouldn't be able to pull them up for quite a ways. I'd just have to drive them, if I could, until they had their run out.

Just before we busted over the hill, I remembered my passenger. She was my passenger now, my responsibility. It was my chore to get her safely out of this predicament, if possible.

I leaned over the side of the coach to see how she was doing, and Time stood still! I looked into the most beautiful sight I had ever seen. Deep green eyes and brilliant flowing red hair blazed up at me and engulfed my very being. In that instant, I knew I was looking at the purest, bravest, most trusting woman that could ever be.

Nanette was by far the most beautiful woman I had ever seen. She never said a word, but in the instant our eyes locked, she seemed to thank me with her entire heart and soul, trusting me for coming to her rescue.

I was spellbound! It seemed like ages that I simply sat and stared; but I know that I could not have hesitated for more than an instant before shouting, "Get inside and hang on!"

In that pause in time, my whole way of life had been shaken to the core. It seemed like I lived a whole lifetime. I was faced with a terrible nightmare. The thought of missing a curve and rolling that coach over the boulders to Kingdom Come, made shudders run down my back, and almost froze me to the lines.

I knew not what the road over the hill was like; but I did know, come Hell or high water, I had to get those racing horses under control, get them pulled up and the coach stopped, all in one piece. That face, engraved forever, on my mind, was trusting in me.

The crest of the hill was almost here. I had the lines straightened out in my hands now, driving those horses bronco fashion, where I could work each individual line between my fingers as needed. Work one in, let slack slip out on another. Six lines to talk to those charging horses, pulling with each one and tugging at the corners of their mouths, trying to tell them to give a little this way or that; most of all, telling them with all my will to pull up, pull up! I could begin to rein them some to right and left now, in the road, but I couldn't slow them down a bit. Had the rocks not been so bad alongside the road, I would have tried to circle them out into the sagebrush, but as rough as it was, it surely would have flipped us. I had my foot on the brake putting all the pressure the coach would stand. Without a load, if I pushed too hard, the rear wheels would lock up, and I could feel the coach start to skid sideways; then I'd have to let up a little. I was getting better response from the horses, but I still couldn't slow them down, no matter how much I see-sawed on the lines and pulled in.

I decided the only possible way I could get stopped before going over the hill would be to shoot the wheel horses and hope their weight dragging in the harness would pull the others down. As close as they were ahead of me, it would be tough to do, what with the coach swinging and swaying, and the horses bobbing around. I would have to try for a head or neck shot so as to drop them as quick as possible. Deciding to try it, I laced the right hand lines through my fingers and up over the thumb of the left hand, to keep the lines straight, and still be able to pull up on all of them.

My right hand swept down to my hip, and then I froze. For an instant I turned so weak, I almost lost everything. My holster was empty! Somehow in the fall back there off Blizzard, I had lost my old revolver. I had packed that gun for years on the range, with horses bucking and falling, and just about everything else you could think of; and it had never gotten away from me. Now I really needed it, and it was gone.

By the time I had the lines back in both hands and straightened out again, we were up to where I could see over the hill and out in the valley below.

It has always been a thrill to me to ride out on the crest of a valley and gaze at country I'd never seen before. This time was no exception, regardless of the circumstances. It was magnificent!

It was miles across the valley. There was a brilliant green spot and a streak of a lake across the valley. It was so far that it almost looked like it was raised back up to my elevation. The ridges in the distance heading up out of the valley were capped with timber.

Off to the left was a "jimmycane', the old desert whirly-wind. It seemed to be standing almost perfectly still, but was carrying a dust funnel thousands of feet into the heavens.

The beautiful picture was completed by the view of a ranch in a grove of poplars at the mouth of a canyon. Across the valley and some off to the right, the road ran straight as a string for miles.

During that quick view of the valley, we'd rushed on far enough to give me a glimpse of the road down to the valley floor. If it was possible, my heart sure pounded even faster. That "road" was nothing but curves, switchbacks, and dips as far as I could see! How in the world I could keep that coach on that goat trail, I couldn't imagine; but I had to.

I've never been very religious, but I've always had my own belief. I came as close to praying that day as I ever have. All I could remember thinking was that those old Abbot-Downing coaches were made to take an awful beating. So maybe if the lady didn't get thrown out, with the Grace of God, she might still be alive when we slung off into space on one of those switchbacks down below.

I'm not trying to say how brave I was, setting up there trying to drive that coach down off that grade. I was just so busy with the reins and brake lever, that it never occurred to me I was in any danger. To say I was busy is putting it mildly.

Not knowing the road, I held the horses to the center of it as we broke over the crest. Luckily the first curve was a gentle one to the right, and it gave me a view of the next one which was the first switchback to the left. The hill didn't appear to be real steep, other than when we first broke over. Right at the top, it dropped out from under me so fast, it took my breath away, and almost lifted me off the seat. When it leveled off almost as sudden, the front of the coach dipped down so low, so fast, I thought we were going end over end right on top of the horses. I had the lines clear up over my head, trying to haul the slack in; and I was down as low as the wheel horses' rumps. It was a good thing we didn't have a sharp curve right there, what with that coach swaying and pitching and bucking; dropping right down on those horses, scaring them to run even faster for a ways.

I had things about halfway back under control by the time we approached the first switchback. I could see it wasn't real sharp, but still, those coaches were designed for gentle curves and straight roads; not sliding around hair pin curves on downhill mountain grades.

The horses were responding to the lines pretty good now; so I was able to hold them to the high side of the curve. As we got into it, I pulled in on my near leader, holding the swing and wheel horses straight across the curve behind the leaders and applying the brake real hard. It locked up the rear wheels, and I was able to throw the rear of the coach into a broad skid and sling it around in line behind the front wheels and the horses. That gave me a good shot at the rest of the curve. The coach was half way turned, but still at the top and to the inside, giving me a straight shot down across the inside of the hairpin, and a chance to complete the curve without skidding off the edge.

Now we were on the straight part between curves again. The horses were giving to the bits real good now, and acted like I might be able to pull them up, if I could get the coach slowed down, but something was wrong. I had my foot on the brake and was pushing down as hard as I could, but it didn't seem to make much difference. Something must have broke or bent out of shape. I could push the brake lever clear ahead, but the brake shoes weren't dragging on the wheels at all.

It was a little ways on to the next curve, and we were slowing down some. The driving strain had eased up, and I had time to look at the road and notice what good shape it was in. It looked like it had just been graded. I guess that movie outfit had worked on it.

All this time, I was see-sawing the horses back and forth, and at the same time kicking the brake on and off, trying to get it to turn loose and start working, in case it was just hung up some way.

It may sound strange, but my mind jumped back to those days in Yellowstone Park, when Sandy and I were chasing Monte, and hauling dudes around in the big sight-seeing coaches. How we used to have stagecoach driving contests at every chance. Pounding down that desert grade with those scared horses and no brake made me think to myself, "Sandy sure outdid me in the romancing; he won Monte fair and square. But lucky for me, I won the stagecoach driving contests.

My last thought before coming to the next curve was , "Well Booger Red, now's your chance to prove you won those contests fair and square."

The grade started to level out, and this curve was a whole lot easier looking, but it must have been deceiving. I had the coach as far to the left as possible, and pulled the leaders in to cut across to the inside; then held in a straight line to the outside again. For a minute, I had my doubts if we were going to make it, coming out of the curve. That old coach leaned so far to the left, that even with my left foot braced solid, it almost moved me across the seat. I heard later that when the movie crew that was trying to catch us got to that point, they could find only one set of tracks around the bottom half of that curve.

The one thing that probably helped us was that when I felt the coach leaning so hard, I quit pulling back on the lines. Going downhill running like that, I hated to ease up any, but that's just what I did, and I squalled at the horses to boot. The sudden burst of speed those horses showed, is what jerked that coach back down on all four wheels. We were on the very edge of the road, swaying and bucking, when we finally got out of that curve, but Luck was still with us. The next time I tried the brake lever, I could hear and feel it take ahold, and slow us down some in our mad pursuit.

Little by little we were easing up; so by the time we hit the last curve, which wasn't bad at all, we just sailed around it in a good gallop and came out onto the straight-away. It was just a short ways more downhill to the desert floor.

Now, up ahead, I could see a building. It appeared to be a mock stage station that I suppose the movie company had built. It looked like people and cameras all over the place. I let the horses canter the last hundred yards into their midst. When their hostlers ran out, I hauled in hard on the lines and yelled a long "Whooooooah!" We came to a stop; dust, lather, horse sweat, and all!

Apparently the movie crew there on the flats didn't realize anything had happened. Not that I expected any attention, but it seemed no one realized I wasn't the regular driver.

I held onto the lines, with my foot on the brake, and watched over the side until my passenger was safely out of the coach and on the ground. As I started to climb down, she turned and looked directly at me. She didn't say anything. She looked sort of pale, but she smiled up at me, and her eyes seemed to say. "Thank you." Then she was gone.

When I climbed off the stage, I noticed several saddled horses tied over to a corral fence. There wasn't anyone close to them, so I picked one out, mounted him, and rode away in a walk. I guess no one noticed me. There wasn't any commotion, and nobody followed me. I had to get back up on the ridge and find out how bad my old grey horse got hurt in the fall he'd taken.

I stayed in the tall brush and cactus back to the hill; then worked my way up a draw to the top before going back to the road. I thought I might find my revolver if I looked around where we'd gone down.

The sign was easy to read. The marks were all there in the dust. Someone had gotten off a horse and picked a revolver up out of the dust, before going on.

The marks of the fall were just beyond, and I could see where a horse had turned back to the desert and was traveling on three legs.

I followed those tracks and found my riata quite a ways on further. Coming over a rise, I saw him laying there. I knew it was going to be bad, because I had been seeing blood all the way; too much blood.

He was still alive when I rode up and dismounted. He raised his head a little when he heard me. Sort of pointed an ear my way; then nickered so soft I barely heard it.

I don't know how long I sat there in the sand and held his head, talking soft to him; trying to comfort him. There was nothing else I could do. His leg was all busted up and jerked out at the joint. He was almost gone when I got there. The last of his gallant life ran out there on the desert sand, while I cradled his head in my arms.

When his eyes finally glazed over, if ever a grown man had the right to lay down and cry, I could have.

I never even had a shovel to bury him with. After unsaddling him and switching my saddle for the one on the borrowed horse, I started to cover him up. I packed rocks, for how long, I do not know. I was so tired I could no longer think. Finally completing the best I could do for the only pard I'd had for many years, I stumbled to my borrowed horse and crawled on him. I just let him go. I had no idea which direction we were going or where. I just didn't care. We'd travel for awhile; then stop for awhile. All night, we kept moving on, here and there.

The sky was still black when my borrowed horse stopped. I could smell and hear water, and see grass all around. I fell to the ground, with one rein wrapped around my hand, and passed out in an exhausted sleep.

Chapter V

LOST CANYON AND THE BRONCOS

Daylight found me sitting close to a small fire, pondering my fate. Things looked pretty bleak. I'd been ordered out of the country. I'd lost my last true friend in the world. Blizzard and I had been so close together for so long. Now he was gone.

I'd lost my sixshooter. True, I did still have the 30.30. and some shells. Maybe I could get an antelope or a deer to survive on. I had a little money in my pocket, but it might be several days ride to the closest town, even if I knew which direction to ride; which I didn't.

It looked like the best thing for me to do now would be to scout the country as soon as it was light enough. Maybe I could find some kind of game and then plan from there.

As it grew lighter, I realized I was in a canyon of some size. There was a little seep in the bottom of the valley. There was a good possibility I'd find fresh water by riding up country.

By the time the sun had climbed up over the canyon rim, I had located the spring. It was an oasis for sure. From the large number of wild animals that arrived there ahead of me, it appeared that it might be the only water for quite a distance.

The morning breeze was drifting down the canyon towards me, so my approach wasn't announced. I spotted the spring from quite a ways off, so I stopped and tied my horse in the brush. Taking the 30.30., I eased up toward the spring.

A beautiful spike buck came out to greet me. He was so

unconcerned by my approach that I had to get ahold of myself to keep from throwing a rock at him to warn him away. I watched him and the other animals for a long time before I finally raised up and dropped him with a shot to the head.

That canyon hadn't been hunted much. The shot hardly bothered any of the other inhabitants. I slipped from cover, and got my buck. Dragging him back a ways from the spring, under a large pinon, I dressed him out.

I had him hung up and almost dressed out when something about the lay of the land beyond the tree caught my interest. At first, it looked like the canyon wall sloped right up to the distant rim, from just beyond a clump of brush. After studying it for awhile, I decided there must be another little side pocket in the valley before that wall shot up to the rim.

I wasn't in any hurry to move out of the country, as I really didn't have anywhere to go. Since it would take awhile to jerk that deer meat, I decided I wanted to look over this valley good before I pulled out. It appeared to be a fairly small basin; one that probably had been overlooked by the ranchers in the area because it was so far off the beaten path, and away from the good ranch country.

After a breakfast of fresh deer liver seasoned with a little rock cow salt, I started on an exploration trip of the basin.

The sun had climbed way up in the sky by the time I'd finished breakfast. I was getting pretty thirsty, so the first place I went was back to the spring for a drink.

The animals had all retired to the shade of their day-time retreats. As I neared the spring, my interest really perked up. There was fresh tracks all around the spring. Fresh horse tracks! Fresh barefooted horse tracks. Maybe five or six head. And they had been made since I had shot the buck, and while I was having breakfast.

They had to be mustang tracks. This was a big open country, and no ranch horse would be ranging out here, unless they'd escaped from somebody's remuda. Six head. Hmmnn. Maybe that was the six head I'd been hunting. The ones that got away from the 2-Bar.

92

They were supposed to be blooded horses. And young. And the reward was still out for their return. I knew then I would have to look the country over real good and figure how to catch that bunch of horses, even if they turned out to be just plain mustangs.

I went up past my breakfast camp and worked up the ridge that sloped upward from the clump of brush close by. I hadn't ridden very far, before I found there was a pocket or depression in the hillside between the ridge I was on and the canyon rim. Then I saw it. The prettiest, most secluded spot for a hideout camp anyone ever saw. Right there in the middle of it in a clump of pinons was a little square cabin made of logs, rocks, and 'dobe. I sat there, spellbound. I was almost afraid to blink my eyes, lest the cabin would disappear, or maybe smoke would come rolling out of the chimney. Finally I rode down to it, studying the country for any sign of human habitation as I approached. There was none whatsoever. A large pack rat nest on the small front porch told me the owner of the cabin wasn't here, and hadn't been here for quite awhile.

I tied my horse and went in. The cabin was small, but it had been built by a professional. It was tight and in good shape. Plain to see, though, that it had been a long time since it had been lived in, possibly a good many years. There was a small camp cookstove, a table with two chairs, and a board bunk with some blankets still on it. Right there in the middle of the bunk was another large pack rat's nest.

There was an enclosed cupboard on the wall, up behind the stove. When I opened it, I got a pleasant surprise. The cupboard was full of supplies, with no more than a little dust on them. Several large cans with lids on tight, were labeled coffee, flour, salt, sugar, baking powder, beans, pepper, and a few others. Every can was almost full, and their contents seemed to be in usable condition. I could hardly wait to build a fire in the stove and cook up a decent meal for myself.

I was pretty sure this wasn't an ordinary ranch line camp, and that I wouldn't have to worry about getting booted out by some working cowpoke about the time I got it cleaned up and moved in.

I went back outside to scout around the place a little better, before going to work cleaning the camp.

There was a small corral that jutted out from the back of the cabin. In the opening for the gate were three slip poles. The bottom one was broken. It looked like an animal might have broken it crawling out from under it. The back side of the corral ran right along the steep hillside. In that corner, a pipe jutted out of the hill into the corral. Spilling out the end of it was a real small trickle of water, falling into a hollowed out log trough. The water looked good. When I got a handful of it, it was cold and tasted good.

Here was a hideaway camp that suited me perfectly. I figured I might stay there; catch a few mavericks, and start up a little ranch of my own. I didn't have the slightest idea whether it was in Arizona or old Mexico. It sure could have been either one.

Back over against the back side of the cabin was a little lean-to shelter. After checking the water, I walked over to it. It was a horse stall, and beside it was a small store room. The first thing that caught my eye was a thirty gallon iron oil drum with the end cut out. On top of it was a homemade heavy wooden lid which covered it. The drum was almost full of shelled Indian corn under that lid. There was every color of corn there I'd ever seen, and then some.

Also, leaning up against the wall, was quite a few hand tools. An axe, shovel, bar, and handsaw. Boy! Everything I'd need to make a ranch out of this place was right here.

I put my horse in the corral; then went to work cleaning the cabin. After I got the cook stove cleaned out and a fire going, I put coffee on to boil. I hadn't had a cup of coffee in so long, it seemed like ages.

That morning before I left my camp, I'd found a cool shady place where I covered the rest of that deer up with some grass and willow bows to keep it cool, and the flies off. I finally decided to go get it and make jerky out of most of it before it spoiled. I was busy the rest of the afternoon.

Just before sundown, I went for a walk back down toward the spring where I'd shot the deer. I was interested in seeing what all wild animals lived in that valley; so I slipped up to the spring real easy.

Before I got there, I was sure I could hear horses moving around.

It was quite a sight when I peered out through the brush covering the boulders. There were six head of horses; two buckskins, two bays, two grullas. My heart almost skipped a beat. Here was my horses. The ones I'd been hunting. Now all I had to do was capture them.

That would take some doing and some planning. I was careful not to let them see or get wind of me. I sure didn't want to scare them away. I sat and watched them, marveling at their shimmering beauty, until almost dark. After they left the spring, I returned to the cabin to stake my horse out on some feed, and fix my supper.

The next morning I rode out to look over the valley. It was a beautiful wild place, almost a box canyon, with quite a few pinon and scrub trees. I finally decided there might be close to a half section in it, as it seemed to be almost a half mile wide and about a mile long. The first circle of the valley, I rode up the bottom of it, studying the rims on both sides. The whole basin had high and low spots in it, so it was hard to maintain a close view of the rims. After I got to the upper end and figured how much of a box canyon it was, I worked my way up to the rim on a game trail that led through the rocks and out onto the high mesa country. There was some old sign of horses having used that trail to get out of the valley. I could see it wouldn't take much work to block that escape route off.

I climbed to a high point where I could see the country for miles and miles in all directions. The old thrill returned as I reached the top and worked my way back out on the canyon rim. My canyon, "Lost Canyon", I named it later, was about a thousand feet deep, and yet someone standing back from the rim just a short ways would never know it was there.

Halfway around and beyond the canyon, there were mountains of great heights, shimmering in the distance. The patches of timber, cactus, and rock cliffs, and stretches of grey sage, covered here and there with the shadow of a lazy drifting cloud, was an impressive sight. I lingered long, soaking it all up with my senses.

When I turned to look back down in my valley, I thought my eyes were playing tricks on me, as sometimes happens when you look too long at one thing. Occasionally bushes and rocks will seem to take the shape of animals, especially if you're looking for them real hard. That's what I imagined was happening to me, as I again saw that six head of broncos grazing on the slope of the canyon opposite me. They were not more than a half mile away. I just had to trap and catch those horses.

I didn't want them to see me; so I pulled back from the rim and started circling it; to determine how many escape routes there were in it.

Going back down the left rim, I found one more game trail that led through a narrow break in the canyon rim. In a matter of a half hour, I was able to build a stone wall that completely closed up the gap.

When I got to the lower end of the canyon, where it emptied out into the wide flat desert valley, I figured out why my canyon was so unused by the outside world.

The main valley which was below it, was quite a bit deeper, and the entrance into it appeared to lead back into the rim only a short ways, because of a tight S curve. The walls of my canyon were almost straight up and down, and real close there at the entrance. To get down off the rim, I had to work my way off into the main valley; then cut across and climb back up to the canyon rim on the other side, before I could continue the trip around the rim.

It looked to me like I could build a horse tight barricade across the mouth of the canyon in about half a day or less. First of all, though, I wanted to check out the rest of the rim for openings.

There was one other trail out on the west side, which took me an hour or more to plug up. It was getting late when I finally worked back around to the trail in the north end, where I'd first come up. I was already tired and hungry, but set into building a plug in that gap too, after I rode back down through it. By the time the last of the day's light winked out up there on the rim, I had a barricade built that I was sure a horse couldn't climb over. The canyon down below sure looked like a dark pool to dive off into, after being up there on that rim all day,

It was so dark, and the trail down the slope was so steep, that I walked and led my horse quite a ways.

but all my nerves were tingling with delight when I thought about having those broncs almost hemmed in. I was pretty certain that they wouldn't work back down to the lower end of the valley and get away before I could get down there the next morning and build a fence across that last opening.

It was so dark and the trail down the slope was so steep, that I walked and led my horse quite a ways. By the time I finally got down to the level, I thought my eyes were becoming accustomed to the dark because I could see better. Then I glanced up at the sky, and I just stopped and stared. There were a million stars out, bigger and brighter than anything I had ever seen in all my life. The whole sky was almost lit up solidly. It seemed as if I might almost be able to reach up and grab a whole arm full of them.

I spent many beautiful nights in that canyon, but that was the one I'll always remember. I hated for the ride home to come to an end, but the comforts of a good camp and a meal were waiting for me.

I was out early the next morning, headed for the mouth of the canyon, packing the axe, shovel, and bar from the tool shed. I sure wanted to get that lower end boxed up before the horses got wind of me and became uneasy, and started hunting a way out of the valley.

By the middle of the afternoon, I had the lower gap fenced in to suit me. I'd even found enough good cedar poles and posts to build a slip pole gate. I wanted it so I could open up the gap and ride out with my horse herd when the time came.

Now that the canyon was fenced, I didn't have to slip around and try to stay out of sight of the broncs anymore. Actually, now it was time to start showing myself to them; so they could begin getting used to seeing a human again.

My plan to catch them was to build a big lot around the spring. They would have to come into it for water. I hoped that by the time I got the corral completed, they would be used to it enough to come right in for water.

Each day that I worked on the corral, I'd take off long enough to saddle my horse and ride out and locate the broncs. The first few days,

I'd stop off quite a ways and wait for them to spot me. After awhile, I'd gradually start working towards them. I didn't get very close the first couple days before they got excited and ran. After that, though, they must have got to remembering that they had seen mounted horses before, because soon I was able to get up within a couple hundred yards before they started getting uneasy.

I don't think they came into water for two or three days after I started working on the water lot corral. Finally on the third morning, when I returned to work, there was fresh horse tracks around the water. They had come in during the night. That's what they continued doing for the next two weeks, while I finished the water lot and a small round breaking corral on the corner of it.

By the time I had the corrals built, I could almost ride right up to them out on the range. I never chased them or tried to drive them to the corrals.

It had been one heck of a hard job building a corral there with very few poles or posts. I'd had to use rocks, mortaring them with dobe mud for the most part.

The broncs continued coming down to water each night, walking around the new portion of the corral to the opening, which was getting smaller each day.

When the time was right, and I had both the big corral and the small one completed, and I had finally located several good poles to slip in the notches in the opening, I was all set. That night, I went down to the corral after dark, and hid where I could listen for the broncs to come in.

That was a long night. I was worried that those broncs had outwitted me. Maybe they knew what I was up to, and had found a way out of my canyon.

It seemed I had been there for hours, and the sky was starting to get light in the east. I was about to give it up for that night and go home, when I finally realized the light in the east was a late moon coming up, not the dawn. I looked to the north star and the big dipper, and figured out I hadn't been there more than a couple hours. I just needed to hold myself in and settle down for a long wait. I'd worked so hard on getting prepared, I sure didn't want to mess it up right at the crucial moment by getting impatient and showing myself, just as the horses might be trailing in. Besides, the night there in the canyon was becoming a dazzling sight, as the moon crept over the rim, and the soft silvery light slid down the slope and chased the shadows away.

Gradually, the night wore on, to the tune of coyotes calling to each other, and night hawks answering that they were also about.

I was hidden where I could still see both the spring and the corral opening.

The water lot fence was as high as my head, but many deer still bounded over it. Some of them worked around to the opening to come in. There was a steady procession of small animals, until late in the night, when it seemed a warning was given by the nighthawks; then all became quiet. Presently a big old lynx cat slipped warily down to water. The small animals all knew where he was.

As the hours passed, the big dipper marched on its circle around the north star. Morning was drawing near, and I was becoming worried that the horses weren't going to water this night.

I must have dozed off for a few minutes; anyhow, I was suddenly startled into alertness by the sound of two rocks being knocked together. Horses were filing through the gate into the water lot. It was hard to sit still and let them get up to the water before I attempted to slip down to the gap and close it. It seemed as if I was making as much noise as a herd of elephants; but somehow I was able to get all the poles in place without spooking them.

It had taken me over two weeks of hard work to build the corrals and capture that band of horses; but my work had only just begun. Now I had to catch them, halter break them so I could get them staked out on feed while I was gentling and breaking them to ride. After that I could take them back to the ranch, collect the reward, and clear my name.

It was lucky for me that I'd found a long, stout, good grass, "lass rope" hanging over an old saddle there in the shed. Also there had been quite a coil of well rope at the cabin, which still held its strength. I had six hackamore halters made from old sacks and the well rope, and had made several sets of hobbles from deer hide.

After penning the broncos early that morning, I returned to camp and slept a couple hours. Then, after a good breakfast, I headed down to the bronc pen with all my ropes and riggin'. I was anxious to get those horses caught and tied up.

As I approached the corral, six pairs of ears were pointed in my direction. When I led my horse through the gate and put the poles back in place, those broncs all headed for the far side. As I remounted and headed for them, they whirled and kicked, running for the corner, where they bunched up. Whistling and snorting, half of them with their rumps toward me, ready to let fly with lightning hooves; the rest of them peeked over backs or under necks at me, their eyes rolling white, and their nostrils flared.

As I moved in, I studied them. I decided to start with the wildest first and work down to the gentlest. Not that any of them were gentle, but they would vary in their reactions and personalities the same as any six people. I'd watched them enough over the past two weeks to have a pretty good idea of their character. I figured the bigger of the buckskins was probably the toughest horse in the bunch, but one of the grullas was the wildest. He had long ago taken over the leadership of this little band. He was intelligent, high-strung and nervous, and the most apt to break and run. He might try to jump or crash through the gate, or any other idea that a wild horse might get; so I went after him first.

I'd ridden my borrowed horse enough to know he was stout enough to handle anything I undertook, and nothing much seemed to bother him. I've learned since, that most horses used much around movie sets get used to most anything.

The grulla was facing me with his head over the neck of one of the bays. I eased up and flipped out a houlihan, the loop going neat and true around his neck. As the bunch broke to both sides from the whistle of the rope, I turned and dallied and headed away, watching the grulla leap high and come down in a full gallop, going the opposite direction. We were already set up, and when that grulla hit the end of that rope, it was tight as a drum. He flipped ten feet in the air and came down in a heap; but he didn't stay there long. Just as I eased up on the slack, he exploded to his feet and headed for the gate. About twenty feet from it, I busted him again, this time landing him on his side. He stayed down, the rope tight around his neck, and just the way I wanted. As I bailed off and ran down the rope, I pulled a footrope out from under my belt, where I'd stashed it so it'd be handy, but still out of the way. By the time I got to him, his breath was coming in gasps. He was weakening, but was still a long way from being beaten. With the foot rope, I flipped a figure 8 around his front feet and pulled it tight. He struggled two or three times to get up, and each time, I pulled his feet out from under him. After the last time, he was so weak, he lay down, his lungs rattling and his strength gone. Quickly I fished the end of the foot rope between his hind legs, drawing a loop around one, and pulling the three feet tight together, crisscrossing them at the ankles. A couple half hitches and he was pretty helpless. I eased up the saddle horse a couple steps then, to loosen the lass rope and let him breathe easier.

Next, with one knee on his neck, and his head twisted right around with his nose in my lap, I fitted the hackamore on him, which I'd grabbed from the pile beside the fence. When it was snug, I ran the lead rope around a stout corral post, carrying the extra coils back with me. He still lay there gasping, while I loosened the foot rope and stepped into my saddle. Dallying with the lead rope, I moved in toward him. As he got his wind back, he began to kick. Realizing his feet were free again, he bounded up with a loud squall and dashed for the fence. Riding crossways toward him, I headed him for my snubbing post and took up the slack as he neared it. Then I spurred hard, whipped around behind him and had him pulled tight to the post before he knew what had happened. Going on to a second post, I tied the halter rope solid.

"There my pretty pidgeon, let's see you fly now."

102

And from then on, I called him Pidgeon.

Knowing he could not get away and had little chance of getting hurt, I left him to fight the rope as much as he wanted. I turned to the others, my attention already on the big buckskin.

Again, I got what I needed ready for the next horse and rode toward the bunch. They broke and split around me, and I let fly at that buckskin as he thundered by. He ducked and I missed. Coiling up my rope, I followed. When he tried to dodge by me again, I got a clean shot, the rope settling right behind his ears. He ran to the end and reared up as he felt it tighten. It pulled him over backwards, his feet thrashing wildly. He was beginning to choke now, so I turned to drag him before he could get back to his feet; but he rolled like a cat and came back up on all fours. His mouth open and big white teeth reaching, he charged at me like a stallion. I jabbed the spurs in that "movie" horse and we stampeded in the opposite direction.

"I'll knock your damn head off," I yelled, as I picked up the slack and took my turns again. He hit the end like a pistol shot and went sailing through the air. When he came down, I dragged him the length of the corral, hoping it would choke him down enough to be able to work on him. I looked back just as the rope gave suddenly, and here that damn cat-footed horse was rolling to his feet again. We turned and raced away again, pulling that rope tight enough to sing, with that buckskin fighting every step of the way. As his wind lessened, he gradually slowed until he was standing spraddle-legged, his head hanging, as he fought for each little breath of air; but he wouldn't go down. I'd known he was tough, but I finally had to turn and ride around behind him and trip him like a steer, to keep him from dying on his feet.

It took me just a few seconds to get his feet tied; then I loosened the rope so he could breathe again. Grabbing another hackamore, I repeated the process as on Pidgeon. He was still whistling through his nose when I untied his footrope, but he lunged to his feet so quick I barely got in my saddle in time. It took another half hour to get that horse worked up close to the snubbing post and tied to my satisfaction.

He was so quick-footed, and the way he glared at me, he sure made me think of a great big yella tomcat.

The next three weren't quite so tough nor as wild as Tomcat and Pidgeon. I finally got them snubbed and tied fast, and noticed that the day was fast ending.

I still had the little bay horse left. He actually wasn't so little, probably fifteen hands and weighed 1,000 pounds, but he was smaller than the others. He hadn't shown nearly the fight the others had, and his eyes had a softness the others lacked. When I roped him, I realized he'd been "started", as he gave to the rope. Talking gently to him, I was able to hobble his front feet and tie up a hind foot, and put his hackamore on without having to choke him down.

I was too tired and stove up that evening at dusk, as I finished tying up the last horse, to cook myself any supper. I ate a chunk of cold meat and fell over on my bunk asleep.

It had been quite a day. Those horses were big and stout and not a bit afraid of me. I had to choke every one of them but one down at least two times in order to get them tied to where I could get the hackamore fitted to them. Then I'd have to drag them to a stout place in the corral to tie them up.

It would have been easier to have forefooted them and tied them up, but they were so stout and active, when I'd forefoot them, I couldn't keep them down long enough to get them tied.

Early the next morning, they were all still tied and standing when I went to check on them. I got my saddle horse and proceeded to drag and lead them one at a time to water. They wouldn't hardly drink, but it was good schooling for them. I spent the afternoon cutting six arm loads of grass and packing it to them. They wouldn't eat either, but I put the grass up where they could reach it, and the next morning it was all gone.

That day they were glad to drink. Already they were starting to gentle down and get used to being handled by me. I started in to breaking them by tying up a hind leg and sacking them out and saddling them.

I put in another hard two weeks, what with batching and hunting grass for those horses, besides working with all six each day. I had them where I could stake them out inside of a week; and in two weeks, I loose hobbled them and turned them out at night to graze.

My supplies were limited, but I had plenty of meat and salt. Also, that barrel of Indian corn in the lean-to had come in real handy. Each day I gave each horse a small handful of it. That wasn' t much, but it was a daily evening-time reward for them.

It was hard to keep track of time, but as near as I could figure out, a month after I corralled those horses, I had them all gentle and pretty well broke to ride. I was about out of grub and was almost to the bottom of the grain barrel. I decided it was time to throw a pack together of the remaining grain and grub, and head out of the canyon. I'd get my bearings, and then aim for the 2 Bar Headquarters with the horses.

I thought the grain barrel seemed pretty heavy to be so low on grain, when I picked it up to pour the last of the corn out into a sack. Just a little grain ran out; then there was a thump, as something in the bottom of the barrel fell over and slid out, and I tipped the barrel clear over.

A leather bag slid out onto my pile of grain.

I stood there looking at it, stupefied for a minute, before I realized the implication. When I picked the bag up and turned it over, it felt quite heavy, maybe twenty pounds or more. The top was squashed down and tied shut with a draw string. I couldn't get the knot undone, so finally took my knife and cut the string. I was sure I had heard a muffled clinking sound come from the bag when I'd turned it. When I pulled the top open, all I could do for awhile was stare. Twenty dollar gold pieces! A whole sack full of them!

I found a clear spot, sat down, and gently poured the sack full of double eagles out on the ground. They sure were beautiful. Slowly I started picking them up and counting them as I put them back in the bag.

There was over 500 of them in that bag.

I never found out who had lived in that camp, or where the money came from. But as remote as the canyon was, and with all the outlaws that roamed that country, I felt it was fruit of the game. There was no way to trace or prove where it might have come from. To me it was "finders keepers", and a new lease on the future.

I was a pretty rough-looking sight that day I left my canyon. My clothes and boots were worn into rags. I whetted up my pocket knife and shaved and washed, and patched my clothes the best I could. I was ragged, but clean; and I sure had a proud string of goodlooking, well started young horses.

With that stake in my pack, my spirits were on the uprise.

If I just hadn't lost my old Blizzard horse; but then, that's Fate.

Chapter VI

THE COW BOSS

That morning when I rode out of my Lost Canyon, I was burdened with a hard decision. Though I didn't know exactly where I was, I knew it wasn't very far to the Mexican border. In two or three days of hard traveling, I could be across the line. With seven good geldings and over $ 10,000.00 worth of gold in my pack, I could go back to the Mexican ranch, claim Lolita, buy some land and a herd of cows, forget about everything that had happened in the States, and be really well off.

I have often wondered why I didn't do things that way.

I guess it was partly because half the cowboys in that part of Arizona had spent some time out hunting those colts and hadn't found them.

I was a stranger that had been accused of cattle rustling. Not only had I found the horses, but I had them pretty well broke to ride. I wanted to return them to their home, claim the reward, and maybe take a chance on strutting a little in front of that damn Mex, Rodriguez. I was sure he didn't know my looks well enough to recognize me. Afterwards I could drift on down Mexico way and look up Lolita.

I had an idea the 2 Bar Headquarters lay to the southwest of my Lost Canyon. I headed east in the main canyon and started working towards high open country.

The broncs had been worked so hard for the past month, they were easy to handle and hold together.

I finally came to a swale high up on the side of a hill, filled with good grass. The horses were more than glad to stop and graze; so I left them and rode on up to the top to study the country. Way off to the southeast, I spotted the two peaks that were out a ways from the headquarters. I still didn't know where I was, but I wasn't lost anymore.

I picked up my broncos and headed on.

It was getting along toward evening, and I still had quite a ride on to the ranch. Early in the morning would be a better time to ride in than at night; so, when I came by a windmill with a small lot fenced around it, I camped for the night.

Ordinarily, I am a very light sleeper. Usually the slightest foreign noise will awaken me. I must have been worn out dead tired that night. Not a sound bothered me. It was after daylight when I was aroused with the feeling another person was there. Maybe I was dreaming, but the feeling got through to me. I was suddenly wide awake, with every nerve in my body on edge. I didn't think I had made the slightest move to indicate I was awake, but I must have done something to give myself away. Before I had my eyes open, I heard the distinct sound of the hammer of a rifle being clicked back to the firing position. At the same time, the words from a Mexican burned in my ear.

"Lay still, gringo, or I'll drill you!"

There he sat on his horse, with that rifle pointing straight at me, when I opened my eyes. The only chance I had was to do exactly what he said.

I was ordered to get up and get my boots on, and to stay away from my rifle.

This Mex was riding a 2 Bar horse, so I pressed the situation by asking him, "What's up? Why are you holding the rifle on me?"

"Don't try to get funny with me, gringo. You think you are so smart. You should have left the country after we caught you stealing the calf. Now we've caught you stealing horses. Soon as Tony gets back with Rod and some more of the crew, we'll cook your bacon, horsethief!"

I tried to tell the Mex I was taking these broncos to the headquarters, but I couldn't talk to him.

He said they'd spotted me the day before, and that if I had been heading for Headquarters, I would have taken the left hand fork of the trail back up the country about five miles. The trail I was on bypassed the headquarters and headed straight for old Mexico.

We didn't have long to wait until Rodriguez and two other vaqueros rode up.

As soon as Rod rode up, I could see his eyes light up when he spotted my bronco herd. He studied them, looking each one over closely before he turned to me.

"Well, gringo," he snarled, "I see you located my broncos, and it looks like you got them broke out for me. Only we caught you before you got away with them. Get saddled, gringo, we'll just help you haze them on over into Mexico; then we'll take care of you and the broncos too."

Things didn't look good for me, with those four Mexes all armed. I didn't have a chance to get away.

When I got my horse saddled, Rod told one of the others to take the lead. Then, turning to the one who had been guarding me when I awoke that morning, he gave him orders to keep his rifle on me and plug me if I tried to escape. He said that he and the other one would ride along and turn the broncs if they started in the wrong direction.

We hadn't ridden very far until the country started to change. We came into a narrow valley that raised up through a narrow pass in the hills.

I was at a real disadvantage, in country I didn't know. Either the Mexes were trying to get me to break and run so they would have an excuse to shoot me, or else they were sure I couldn't get away from them. In any event, I wasn't tied in any manner. I was really studying the country close, up ahead, looking for an escape route.

For an instant I was positive I saw the sunlight glint off a rifle barrel up ahead in the pass. The Mexes weren't worried so they weren't watching closely.

111

We were well up in the pass when the quiet of the canyon was suddenly shattered by the explosion of a repeater rifle cutting loose.

Those broncs whirled and swept around me in a dead run, carrying me back with them down the trail we'd just come up. The three Mexes behind me ducked behind some rocks at the side of the trail at the sound of the shots. They seemed to be having a little disagreement as we swept by. We were a mile or more back down on the flat before they began to slow down, and I was able to get them under control to where I could drive them again.

I continued jogging back up the country, all the while looking back over my shoulder. Nothing showed up. It sure was quiet.

I worried about whoever it was that had fired the shot which had enabled me to get away. I reasoned out that he had gotten there ahead of us; so he probably had it figured out how he could get back out on his own. Also, I didn't have a gun. That was the one thing the Mexes had taken from me.

I decided that I would keep on going up country, hurrying as fast as possible, and take the other fork of the trail that led to the 2 Bar headquarters. If Rod rode back there, I'd be there first; but I bet with myself that he wouldn't show up again.

It wasn't long after I headed down the left fork before I came to a road I recognized. I knew where I was then, and it wasn't far on to the ranch. Just then I spied a horseman quartering in toward me from my right. For a minute, I had to control my impulse to keep from bolting into a dead run and try to get away. That just had to be that Rod guy.

When he got a little closer, I could see this rider was too large for the Mexican. What a relief!

As he came trotting across the flat toward me, that rider sure looked like an Oregon buckaroo, from the style of his riding and the way he was sitting his saddle.

Then I recognized him as the old "P" Ranch cowboy. I hated to think of him as a choreman. He had too much class for that, but anyway that's who it was. I wondered what he was doing way out here, ahorseback; and then I saw the rifle butt sticking up out of his riggin', and instantly I knew. He had been the hidden rifleman over in the pass leading to Mexico.

The broncos reached a little patch of grass up ahead and stopped for a snack; so I pulled up and waited.

"Hello, Old Timer. Thanks for the help over the hill there."

He waved a hand to pass it off, and came back with, "Was glad I could help. Only wish I could still see good enough to have drilled that Mex instead of just winging him."

"How'd you happen to be there at the right place? You sure saved my bacon", I replied.

He went on to tell me about having a young milk cow that was due to calve out, that he was worried about. He'd gotten up in the middle of the night to go check on her. When he saw the vaqueros catching fresh horses and saddling them, he'd become suspicious. He'd slipped around to where he could hear them talking and had learned of their plans. He'd thought of trying to get some help to come to my rescue, but was afraid something would go wrong. He was sure the Mexes would take that route across the line, and that he could stop them. We were lucky, the way the broncs had doubled back past me. That created enough instant confusion to open an escape route for me, and allow the old timer to slip back to his horse and ride back across the mountain.

"Pop" was what everyone on the ranch called the old Oregon buckaroo. He went on to tell me that he'd been suspicious of Rodriguez for a long time. From what he'd heard there in the night, Rod apparently had stolen those young horses and had put them up in that canyon, wherever it was that I'd found them. He'd just been waiting for the right time to get them and move them on to Mexico.

Pop had really taken a shine to me, probably mostly because I was from his home range. It was about time I found another friend. I sure needed one.

We'd ridden along quite a ways when Pop came out with, "By golly, Red, I see you've even got those colts all broke to ride. How are they?"

I enjoyed the next half hour, talking about the broncs and telling

Pop what good horses they were. He knew the big boss would be pleased to have them back, and was sure to give me an extra bonus if they were all broke out good and gentle.

We rode into the ranch yard just as a cowboy crew was mounting up to come hunt for the mysterious disappearance of Pop. The young milk cow had gotten out and run off down in the willows somewhere to have her calf. It was past noon and Pop hadn't been seen since the night before, and his horse was gone.

Since Rod and three of his men were also gone, nobody had the slightest idea whether they were together or not; so the jigger boss had decided it was time they went looking.

Needless to say, they were quite surprised when Pop and I drove those broncos into the ranch and corralled them.

The crew was all curiosity, and wanted to know why Pop hadn't left word what he was up to.

Pop pulled a surprise on all of us then, when he came out with his story.

"Boys," he started, "I've got quite a yarn to tell you all, but first off, I want to introduce you to a friend of mine from Oregon. Boys, this is Booger Red," and "Red", he continued, looking at me with a twinkle in his eye, "Everyone of these boys here are cowboys and good ones. There isn't a man here you couldn't ride the river with."

All was quiet for a minute. It embarrassed those cowboys to be bragged on. I just raised a hand and waved a friendly acknowledgment of them in acceptance of Pop's statement.

"I've been working on something but I wasn't free to tell you before, but I guess now's the time to do it."

Mr. Tom, your boss here, and I are old friends from a long time ago. His daddy sent Tom out to work for me and learn the cow business when I was running a cow outfit up north. Tom was a green kid, fresh out of college when he got there, and the crew sure gave him a rough time for awhile; but he had spunk and stuck it out. He stayed there until he became a top hand, good enough for anybody's outfit, before he struck out on his own.

114

A couple years back I ran into him at the Denver show. We hadn't seen each other for years. After several days visiting, and Tom learned I wasn't working anywhere, he told me about some problems he was having down here. He asked me to come here and piddle around the ranch and see what I could figure out. The choreman's job was a perfect cover, and gave me something to keep busy at.

I know all you boys appreciate Rodriguez for the cowboy he is, and I sure hate to tell you this, but I became suspicious of him right from the start. We never became friends, and he has tried to run me off for a long time.

Red, here, came by a couple months ago, wanting to know if the reward was still good on those horses. He'd seen an old poster on them. He said he was going out on the range to locate the six head if they were still in the country.

Last night, when I became uneasy about that young milk cow, and went to check on her, I stumbled into some interesting news. Rod, Tony, and Jose were saddling horses, getting ready for a little midnight ride. I dropped down and listened to them discussing their plans. Pancho and Tony had spotted Red trailing the broncos home yesterday. He'd stopped at the government windmill last night to camp. Pancho had stayed out there to guard him, and Tony brought the news to Rod.

Rod and his boys planned to drive the broncos, along with Red, over into Mexico, where they'd finish Red off. They had a market for the horses further south.

Well, after they left, I did a little riding of my own. I waited for the bunch of them over in the pass to Mexico and spoiled their plans. I unlimbered that rifle of mine and let 'er fly. I winged Pancho, and the broncos darn near turned somersaults heading back down the trail. They carried Red back down from the pass with them, as the Mexicans high-tailed for the brush. I slipped out the other way and cut across the top. Met Red down the trail a ways and here we are."

There were a bunch of questions asked by the crew about where I'd located the horses, and how I'd caught them. None of the crew knew about my Lost Canyon.

We stood there toe to toe, and traded slugs, with neither one of us trying to block the other's blows, for ages, it seemed like.

Finally one of the boys came up with the fact that now the ranch didn't have a cowboss, since Rodriguez was outlawed. Here Pop spoke up again.

"I've had Tom convinced for quite awhile that Rod was the cause of all his problems here. Last week before he left to go take care of some other business, he told me that if anything happened while he was gone that I was to take over; and if I knew of a man to take Rod's place, that I had the authority to hire him. Well, boys, to make it short and sweet, Red is the new cow foreman here; so if any of you disagree with my judgment, now's the time to sound off. Red, here, can answer your questions."

There wasn't a sound for a few minutes. The crew all seemed to look at the ground for awhile; then they all kind of glanced toward the jigger boss. Finally one of them says, "Tex, what do you think of this yarn?"

"I'll tell you what I think," he snarled, "There ain't no two bit four -flushing logger from Oregon going to step in here ahead of me and take the job I've worked my hind end off to get. I'm the jigger boss here, and you guys'll take your orders from me 'till Tom gets back and tells these "buckaroos" what's up. And besides, I want to know how come this jasper here's riding a 2 Bar horse!"

Pop had dumped the cowboss job on me, if I was man enough to handle it. It sure sounded good to me. My answer was made with action, and damn fast.

I'd had my riata down, showing it to Pop on the way in. Instead of strapping it back on my saddle, I'd just hung it over the horn with a couple of coils in a loop on the top.

When Tex blowed up and bucked Pop's statement, I got a little irritated, and decided that if nothing else, I was going to have a try at teaching him to say, "Yes Sir." When he wanted to know about the horse I was riding, I already had my answer coming. In one motion, I grabbed that riata and shot a Houlihan loop at Tex that settled down over his head and over both arms to his elbows, faster than a diamondback's strike. I spun a turn on the horn as I was reining and

117

spurring my horse away from the cowboy group. The results were that Tex's arms were pinned to his body and he was jerked out of the saddle before he had time to quit talking. I dropped the coils of my riata and hung my reins over the saddle horn and stepped off before Tex could get to his feet. As I was stepping over to him, I threw a quick glance at the rest of the crew. Pop was there on his horse facing them, with his rifle out and pointing in their direction. In that instant before the storm broke, I could hear him saying, "Easy, boys, stay out of it."

Then Tex and I came together.

He was a little older and bigger and meaner than I was, but I knew it would be a battle to the finish between him and me; so I was willing to give him back as many dirty tricks as I could when he used them on me.

When I got up to him, he was back on his feet with his arms in the air, throwing the rope off his head.

I didn't wait for an invitation.

I just bored in and went to slugging right in his exposed middle. I got in two or three good hard pile-driving punches before he came unwound, and that he did! We stood there, toe to toe, and traded slugs with neither one of us trying to block the other's blows, for ages it seemed. Man, that guy could hit! I guess we each had the same idea that we could punch the other man out in a hurry and get it over with, but we had about met our equals. We were both hard punchers, and we both could take it.

How long we stood there pounding each other, I don't know. We both were becoming bloody messes; our knuckles and cheeks, and jaws were peeled wide open. Every nerve and muscle in my body was on edge. I couldn't absorb much more of that punishment, but there was no way I could get away from it either. Then there was a clear opening at the side of Tex's head. I don't know how I got one of my fists back and down so far, but I started that punch from about my hip pocket. I poured every last ounce of my strength in behind it, as it was traveling toward his head. I was in such a fatigued state, that things were running through my mind in slow motion. It seemed like it was taking me forever to land that punch. I wondered why Tex didn't dodge it, as slow as it was coming at him. Then, when it connected, it was like the crushing kick of a jack mule. It seemed that my fist just flattened out as it squashed into the side of his head. The pain shooting all the way back up in my shoulder, sort of snapped me out of my stupor for a spell.

Tex just sort of folded over and backed up and sat down. Then his head and shoulders flopped over between his knees, and he looked as if he was just resting.

I didn't remember it, but Pop told me afterwards, that I turned toward the crew and muttered, "You guys'll have to wait your turn." Then I slumped forward and stretched out on the ground.

The next thing I knew, I was on a bunk, and Pop and another cowboy were doctoring my cuts and bruises. Man, I hurt all over.

I got one eye open and looked around. There across from me, heaped on a bunk, was another cowboy; and a couple fellows were working on him. I went back to sleep. When I woke again, the first thing I saw was a peeled up cowboy propped up on that other bunk. Pop was setting there talking to him.

It was the next day at noon, before Tex and I felt like hobbling out to the cookshack for dinner.

We hadn't been laying in there on our bunks snarling at each other, but we also hadn't done much visiting. I was real surprised when we limped in there and sat down at the table. He stood up and made his spiel. He said, "Boys, this Booger Red here and I had a little chat. He has convinced me that what Pop told us just before the storm hit is the gospel. I suggest we believe what Pop said, and get behind this redhead here, and see if we can't shape him up into a cowboss for us."

A spokesman for the crew stood and says, "Tex, if that's the way you feel, we'll sure agree with you. We weren't particularly looking forward to having the same kind of a chat with him that you did. If we all pitch in, why maybe we can make a half-way decent boss out of the little red-headed booger."

There were some laughs and comments around the table. Then I held up my hand in the Indian peace sign and said, "Thanks, boys, I'm 'bout starved. Let's eat."

Tex was a good jigger boss. He knew the crew and they liked him. He knew the ranch and horses and cows well too. I was surprised that he hadn't been made the cowboss a long time ago, until I learned that he liked to go to town and get tanked up pretty regular.

The first couple weeks there, I told Tex to go ahead with the work like he was the boss, while I followed him around, until I got acquainted with the ranch and crew and horses.

It was a good outfit, close to 10,000 cows. With year round range, that made for a lot of riding. I already had seven head of 2 Bar horses, so I just kept them for my string.

After I'd been with the outfit a couple weeks, most all of us were sitting together at the cookshack one evening after supper. I figured it was about time to answer the question that Tex had asked me that day before our fight; about how I come to be riding a 2 Bar horse. I told them that I had ridden into the country on my own horse, and that he sure had been a good one. While chasing a coyote, he had stepped in a badger hole and broke a front leg, and I'd had to do away with him. I'd walked for the better part of a day when I came on this 2 Bar horse standing tangled up in his reins. He'd had an old saddle on, so I borrowed him, backtracked to where I'd cached my outfit, and then got lost in a storm. I'd blundered on to those broncos in a little canyon off out in the wilds. It was easier to corral the broncs and break them to ride than it was to try to drive them, wild as they were. Especially when I didn't know how to get back here because I didn't really know where I was to start with.

I didn't have any intention of saying anything about the stagecoach runaway I'd blundered into.

I finished my yarn and suddenly noticed the crew had all become almost embarrassingly quiet, like cowboys do when a stranger breaks into their circle.

120

I turned partly around, looking for what had drawn their attention. There stood Pop, grinning as big as you please. With him was a dressed-up rancher looking feller, and between them was what was making the whole crew so self-conscious.

There stood a very beautiful young woman, with long wavy red hair! My knees almost buckled under me as I turned around, and by chance, looked straight into her eyes; deep, warm, green eyes; the same eyes that had spoken "thanks" to me that day as I climbed off the stagecoach!

Pop brought me to reality by saying, "Boys, this Booger Red here, . has just fed you one whale of a big windy. This redhead is the gent that boarded that stagecoach that day on top of the mesa and drove it down off the grade. It was him that delivered our little Nanette here safe and sound down on the flats to the unsuspecting camera crew."

"That's how he lost his 'Blizzard' horse, racing him across that boulder patch, to get to the coach. I rode back up there the next day after Nan told us what happened. I followed the sign out to the pile of rocks, with our saddle on top of it. After that, the trail faded out. Boys, we all owe this Booger Red a bunch", he was saying, as I ducked out the door. I just had to get away from everybody for awhile.

121

Chapter VII

THE ROUND-UP

I'd walked clear down to the bronc corrals and was standing there trying to get my thinking straightened out, when I heard someone, with a voice so soft and sweet and warm, saying, "Mr. Red".

I turned, and there she stood, holding her hands out to me. It just seemed the natural thing to do; for me to take those two hands and draw her almost up to me.

"Mr. Red," she said again, "I have wanted so much to find you since that day, and thank you."

"Getting you down there safely was all the thanks I needed. That almost scared me to death, seeing you in that coach like that."

I didn't try to hug her or anything. We just stood there, smiling at each other, both of us thrilled beyond words that we'd found one another.

"Do you feel like walking for awhile with me?" I asked. I needed to be moving around, but I didn't want to be away from her side.

"All night, if you like," was her answer.

To hear her voice made me like putty in her hands. I asked her to tell me about herself.

"What would you like to know?" were her words.

"Anything and everything," I replied.

"O.K., if you'll tell me about yourself," she smiled up at me; and nodded.

She said, "I'm 21, single, and never met a man that interested me until I saw you racing across the flats on that grey horse that day."

We stopped and turned toward each other again. It was hard to keep from drawing her to me. I couldn't keep from telling her though, "Nanette, you are the wonderfullest girl I have ever met."

She leaned her head against my shoulder, and we stood there that way a long time. Content to be there together without talking.

We finally walked on, and talked; telling little things about ourselves. We climbed up a ridge to a rock outcropping, and there leaned against the rocks and talked more.

Hours later, a sliver of moon came up and lit the trail back down to the ranch for us. It was late, but it seemed we'd only been together a short time when we got back to the ranch house. We were met there by Pop and the other gentleman who'd been with him.

Nanette bid me goodnight, saying she'd see me the next day, and went inside.

Pop says then, "Red, I'd like for you to meet Mr. Tom. My friend, and the son of an old friend, and the man we're working for here."

We shook hands, and Tom spoke right out, saying, "Red, it's pleased I am to meet you. I'm not going to try to thank you for all you've done for us, but I want you to know we sure appreciate it."

"I just happened to be there and glad I could help," was my answer.

We talked about other things, in particular about the strayed broncs; where and how I'd caught them. Tom wanted to know all about my Lost Canyon, and where it was. He said he'd flown over it a time or two, but didn't think it amounted to much. He seemed to think the spring didn't show up from the air, as he hadn't noticed any. He was quite surprised to learn the horses had probably been there all the time.

We discussed the ranch, and the cattle, and the work that needed to be done. Tom had signed a contract to deliver four thousand head of three and four year old steers to some eastern buyers pretty soon. This meant we'd have to get the chuckwagon out and pull out on the range to start the roundup of the steers right away.

That was the kind of work I knew and liked. I was really looking forward to getting on with it, until I thought of Nanette. It might be a month before we'd be back to headquarters, what with the roundup and trailing the steers back to the railroad.

I didn't get much sleep that night. I tried to think of the work involved in getting ready for the coming roundup. We'd have to get the chuckwagon out of the shed, clean and stock it. Look to the brakes, and soak the wheels in linseed oil. Grease the axles. Get the mules in, roach them and trim their tails and shoe them. It wouldn't be a bad idea to hook them to the freight wagon and send some of the boys to the hills for a load of pinon and cedar firewood. We'd have to get the extra horses up and make our roundup remuda. It might take us at least two days to get ready to pull out, or maybe we'd be ready to start on the second afternoon. That would give me at least once more evening to visit with Nanette, unless of course, she left before then to go see some of her town friends. Then all my thoughts turned to her.

I had seen Nanette three times before tonight. It seemed I had known her all my life, Tomorrow morning, she was sure to awaken, glad to think that she had gotten to thank me for helping her that day in the stagecoach, but kind of relieved that her obligation was over. She had seemed so interested in me when we were walking, but surely she was just a warm, loving, friendly type of person; and that was her way of paying me back for helping her. I couldn't imagine a girl like her having any prolonged interest in a wandering cowpoke like me. Now she would be free to go on with her movie career, or whatever else she was after.

And that made me think of Monte. Let's see now, it must be close to a year now, since she and Sandy had gotten married. It was hard to keep track of time, back in those days. The seasons of the year weren't so hard to keep up with if you stayed in one area most of the time, but when you roamed around as much as I had been doing, it was easy to get mixed up. I finally gave up trying to figure what the date was, and just went to figuring on tomorrow.

I'm not sure if I ever went to sleep that night or not. My head was so full of the roundup and Nanette; so mixed up that I almost missed breakfast.

The rest of the crew was already at the table when I rushed in to the cookshack.

I had taken time to wash and comb my hair. Was I glad! There at the table, next to where I usually sat, was Nanette! Smiling up at me, she said, "Good morning, sleepy head. I thought maybe you'd gone to Mexico."

That brought grins from the cowboys.

Nan told me later that I blushed something awful. I probably did, too, as I wasn't used to being greeted that way by pretty girls.

I had a whole sermon prepared for the cowboy crew, with instructions for the coming roundup; but with Nanette there, I found it hard to concentrate on plans for leaving for a month.

Before I'd finished eating, Nan came out with a surprise.

"Uncle Tom tells me you boys are going to start on a steer roundup as soon as you can get ready."

If she didn't have the attention of the whole crew already, this really drew it. That was real cowboy work; what the whole crew wanted.

"Yes," I said, "We got to gather 4,000 head of three and four year old steers for delivery pretty soon."

I looked at her, and would like to have added my thoughts, "I'll sure miss you."

She spoke up again. "Uncle Tom said I could go along, if it's alright with you," looking straight up at me.

I tried to pass the buck by coming out with, "I wouldn't mind, but I'm afraid the crew might feel uneasy with a woman around. You know how we have to camp out in the open so much."

"That's settled then," she grinned at me. "I'll ask them right now."

"Boys, be honest and tell me the truth. You all know I've been on some of the roundups for a few days at a time before. I want to go on this one all the way, but if there's a one of you here that objects, I'll not do it."

Tex settled the issue.

"Miss Nanette, if you bring your tepee along and set it up back out of the way, we'd be tickled to death to have you."

I threw my hands in the air, so thrilled I was about to bust, and grinned.

"You win, Nanette."

Turning to the crew, I said, "Boys, I had a whole sack full of pills to issue this morning, but I'm sure each of you know more about getting ready for a roundup here than I do. So, Tex, you take over and give what special instructions are needed. We'll try to get ready to pull out tomorrow night, and then go on from there."

Tex looked at me with an evil twinkle in his eye, and mentioned that each man usually took four horses on roundup. Adding, that since about all I had was that old 2 Bar dude horse and those broncos, he was wondering if I'd like him to cut me out a couple older circle horses out of the extras. I had been around enough cow outfits to know what he had in mind without looking at him, but I just couldn't help grinning and answering.

"Yeah, some of my colts are pretty much ridden down. Maybe a couple of good, tough, rested, circle horses would be alright to have along."

My broncs were six year olds, in good shape, and tough as whang leather. They didn't need to be laid off for a rest, but Tex just wanted to stake me to a horse and I knew why. He probably had some old gentle horse that was easy to saddle and anybody could get on; but that hadn't been ridden to a standstill in a good many years.

I hadn't exactly whipped him in that fight we'd had, but he would feel a lot better if he could pull a trick like that on me. I tried hard not to let on like I had the slightest idea of what he was up to. Besides it would be fun anyhow.

Nan told Tex what horses she would like to take, and said she'd personally pay $ 1.00 above wages, if any of them needed shoeing, to whoever would do it for her. Half the crew immediately volunteered, each man insisting he was the best horseshoer in the bunch; and not to let the other fella do it because he didn't know a hind foot from a front one. Every man there would have been delighted to do it for nothing, just for the glory of getting special attention from Nan. It wasn't hard to see what a favorite she was among the boys.

The ranch was a busy place that morning. The crew all knew what to do; so it only took a few words from Tex to get things rolling. Three or four of the boys went to gather the extra horses; while the rest of us went to work on the chuckwagon and the mule harness. One man who was also a pretty good blacksmith, stoked up the forge and went to hammering out horse shoes.

Mr. Tom came down in the middle of the morning and mentioned for me to come over and hold a powwow with him.

"Nan says she's going on the roundup", he said, looking straight at me. I nodded my head and he went on.

"She's a good cowboy, and gets kinda wild and reckless at times. Needless to say, I hope you'll look after her, and try to keep her from getting piled and hurt; though Lord knows how anyone could keep her from doing something she set her mind to. I never could."

I really wished she wasn't coming on this roundup because it's no place for a woman. On the other hand, the thought of seeing her every day, was like downing whiskey at one gulp. I couldn't stand the thought of trying to persuade her not to come.

"Mr. Tom," I says, "I'll do what I can to keep her out of trouble."

"Speaking of trouble," Tim grinned, "Nan told me that Tex is going to cut you out a couple 'good stout rested circle horses.' Is that right?"

"Uh huh," I smiled back at him.

"Well, " he says, "I doubt if any of those extra horses are better, or even as good as those broncos of yours. Why don't you just use them on the roundup?"

"Mr. Tom, Pop told me about your younger days, when you came to work for him. He said you were game all the way. Now you wouldn't want to get cautious and spoil all the fun for the crew now, would you? And lose all their respect to boot?"

130

With a twinkle way down deep in his eyes and looking straight at me, he put a hand on my shoulder, and says, "Red, my boy, be careful. Take a deep seat and a long rein; lean way back and let ' er rip!"

Before leaving, he said, "Come up to the house tonight for supper. I want you to meet my wife. And Nan said she'd do the cooking!"

I nodded yes, and stood there with my thoughts as he turned and walked away.

There was a joyous air at the noon-time table. The crew was happy to get back out with the wagon. The boys had gotten in with the extra horses just before the bell rang. It wasn't long before questions were being asked of the boys who jingled the horses about certain ones. How this horse looked? Was old Rock still lame? Had Cimarron's wire cut all healed up? How was Applesauce?

At this last name, all the crew became very attentive.

"All his old saddle marks are all healed up. He's fat and sassy. I'm sure he could stand another roundup," was the reply from one of the horse wranglers.

"Whose string is he in, Tex?" came from another.

"Well, now, let's see," Tex contemplated. "I guess he's in the extra string right now. You know, he might make Booger Red a good night horse. We got quite a few good ones now since Rod and his boys are gone."

"That Frisco horse might be a good one too," someone else chimed in. "Course he's a little tough to shoe." This brought smirks all around.

I ate a light dinner. I was sure that afternoon's chore would be to go down to the horse corrals and work out the roundup remuda. Of course, I'd be expected to try my new horses out to see how they handled.

A meal with a cowboy crew never did take very long to complete. This day it seemed faster than usual.

Pop had a separate small cabin he lived in. Some days he ate with the crew. Some, he ate at his cabin, or with Tom. Some, he done without. This day, he'd come in and ate a little with the crew; then headed back to his cabin.

When I left the cookshack, I headed over there. He was sitting in a straight-back homemade chair, smoking a durham, deep in thought when I came in. Neither of us spoke for awhile. Finally Pop says, "Red, that Applesauce is over fifteen years old. And from what Tom tells me, he's never been rode to a standstill; and lots of good boys have climbed on him."

"I'd hoped maybe he wasn't quite that tough."

"You don't have to try him you know?"

"Don't I?" I asked as we studied each other.

"Don't worry Pop. I'm young and feel pretty good today. So, if you'll lend me that bronc quirt you're fiddling around with, I'll try to give the boys a show."

I tucked the quirt inside my shirt, and went to see about my saddle. I didn't want something breaking.

When I got to the corral, the whole crew was there, along with Tom, Pop, and Nan. As I walked by her, she spoke low for only me to hear.

"Good luck, Red. Be careful. Those boys are full of the devil, and they are going to try to put one over on you today."

I didn't stop, but looked toward her, winking one eye, and said, "They wouldn't do anything like that, would they?"

Two or three of the boys already had horses caught, but they weren't doing anything with them yet. It was easy to see they were stalling so they'd be free to see the fun.

I walked into the horse corral with my riata in my hands, and a heavy hackamore hanging on my left arm.

Tex met me and wanted to know if I had any preference as to size or color, or would it be O.K. for him to pick something that would make me a good dependable mount.

"You know the horses, Tex, why don't you point one out? We got lots of time, so I'll try him, and if I don't like him, we'll go on from there."

I thought he was going to split wide open trying to keep his inner

Once in awhile, when I'd get a view of his head, I'd take a swipe at it, but most of the time, I couldn't keep track of where his head was.

feelings from showing.

"O.K." he says, "There's several here that might do. That big old yella horse there's a good one. No, by golly, he's lame. Well, let's see, that big bay there is sure a good one, but Damn! He's got a wirecut on his fetlock."

I could see it was an old cut and didn't bother him any, but I didn't argue the point.

About that time, this big roan, red and blue speckled like a bird's egg, turned in front of us.

Tex says, pointing, "That old roan, Applesauce, there is a good one. Catch him."

I had a small loop built, and had already spotted the horse I knew he'd eventually pick for me, so I was ready. When Tex says, "Catch him," I pitched out a houlihan and dobbed it around his neck almost before Tex was through talking.

Applesauce was very deceiving. He played right along with those cowboys by turning and coming right up to me, as quick as I jerked my slack. He walked right up with his ears cocked forward as friendly as you please.

I could have sworn there was a smile on his face as he held his head out for me to fit the hackamore on.

I hadn't let on to the crew yet that I was the least bit suspicious, as I scratched Applesauce's ears and smiled at Tex. I commented on what a friendly cuss he was.

"He needs his feet trimmed a bit and his tail pulled some, but I reckon I'll saddle him and lope him around a bit before I clean him up," I says.

"Yeah, that might be a good idea," agrees Tex, so excited he had to look at the ground to keep from giving himself away.

If I hadn't known different, I surely would have been fooled by that Applesauce's actions. You just couldn't have asked for a better dispositioned, friendly horse than what he was. I brushed him down, felt of his back and muscles, and combed a knot or two out of his mane. His body was as solid as iron, and he felt like a keg of dynamite to me.

I took him into a big open corral before I started to saddle him. I never let on like I noticed that the work of the whole crew had ceased, and they were all in remarkably good positions to view what was happening between Applesauce and me.

That old hoss never moved, flinched or puffed up a bit when I saddled him.

I almost hated to go through with what I was about to do, but looks can be deceiving.

When I finished saddling him and had checked my off stirrup; without 'tracking' him, I stopped by his head, and looking him right in the eye, says to him, "I'm sorry about this, Old Timer!" As I slips the quirt out of my shirt, I toes the stirrup and swings in his middle.

I didn't try to ease him out or nudge him or nothing. As I picked up my off stirrup, and my body slid way down deep in my riggin', my boot heels were traveling with all the speed I could muster, up past the point of his shoulders. Then I drove my spurs down and into those shoulders as hard as I could. At the same time, my right arm was making a wild streaking motion down toward his under side, just ahead of his hind legs, with that heavy shot-loaded bronc quirt in my hand, whistling through the air.

I had taken everybody, even Applesauce, by surprise; but not for long! To say he blowed up would sure be under-rating him. That old fool just plain exploded!

He leaped straight in the air, swallowing his head and kicking at my spurs all at the same time. I know we hit the ground ten feet away and headed in the opposite direction before I could quirt him a second time. For an instant, I thought he had got me on that first jump. It made me so damned mad, I really got wicked. I squalled at him with all the might of an old she mountain lion. It startled the old pony so that he hesitated just for an instant, but that was all I needed to catch up with him again. I was kicking and spurring him with all the fury of a mad man, while at the same time, I was quirting him with all my might; first on one side and then down across the other. Once

135

in awhile, when I'd get a view of his head, I'd take a swipe at it, but most of the time, I couldn't keep track of where his head was. He'd just plain fall to pieces one way; then fall right back through himself the other way. One jump he'd hit stiff-legged on his front legs so hard it would almost drive me right down through the saddle; then the next jump he'd land on one front leg while dropping his shoulder with the other, and send the swells of my old hack shooting sideways so hard it would almost rip me apart.

This was the first time in his life he'd ever had a hard time getting rid of his rider, and he was getting worried. I knew something was up as he cocked his head sideways and looked at me at the bottom of another piledriver jump, and I was still there.

I drove my quirt down across the point of his nose and squalled at him as the blood spurted out. We were fairly close to the fence when we came out of that jump. What did he do but just plain dive and fall sideways into the pole fence. Barely in the nick of time, I managed to pick my right leg up and drive my spur into his neck, out of the way of the poles, just in time to keep from getting it crushed. I hit a tender spot, and ripped the hide open and knocked him to his knees. For a minute I thought he was going down, but then he caught himself and lunged to the middle of the corral. In a flash, he throwed himself over backwards. I swung sideways and threwd myself from the saddle and lit on my feet, by his back, still holding the hackamore reins. He spun, trying to paw me and lunged to his feet, but I was too quick for him. I slid back on him as he came up. We made one high wild jump, and then he throwed himself over backwards again.

I managed to step clear of him again. Only this time, when we lit on the ground, I made a wild grab and caught ahold of the rein close to his chin with one hand, and caught a handful of his nose with the other. I had his head twisted with his nose up close by my belt. In a flash, I stood on one foot and went to tromping my very pointed cowboy boot heel into his neck. I tromped as hard and as fast in that neck muscle as I could; then I stood on that foot and tromped with the other foot for a few times, until he was able to jerk out of my grasp.

Again he lunged to his feet, and again I somehow managed to come up with him. We were sort of over at one side of the corral, heading towards the open side of it, as we came up fighting, but it was about over. Something had to give soon. I was getting so weak, I hardly knew what I was doing.

Applesauce was weak also. When he gained his feet, he just sort of reared and took a crowhopping jump straight across the corral.

If you've ever heard anything to chill your blood, it's a horse bawling; and that's what Applesauce started doing while in the air on that jump. He kept it up, crowhopping and bawling for one, two, three more jumps. Then he stopped and stood on spraddled legs, with his head hanging down almost to the ground. There wasn't a sound in the corrals anywhere, except his and my labored breathing.

We sat that way for several minutes. As I regained some strength and looked that poor old broken-hearted horse over, his neck and shoulders and nose was cut to ribbons. Little pools of blood were forming on the ground and running down his legs. The bleeding wasn't serious; it would stop pretty soon, but he sure looked a sight.

Finally I got enough strength to step off him. Standing by his side with my hand on his neck, I looked up. There just a few feet away was Tex, looking very sheepish and wanting to say or do something.

It was time to take over.

"Tex, will you send one of the boys after a bucket of warm salt water and some medicine for me? I'll keep this old horse, but it looks like maybe you better cut me out something else not quite so gentle, to use on this roundup."

Pop hobbled up to within talking range by now. He sure had a bright twinkle in his eye when I looked at him. I asked if he had a feed of grain I could have, and if I could put old Applesauce in his milk cow pasture. Also if he would doctor the old horse for me while we were gone.

"Yes," he says, "and I'll be right back with the grain."

I sure felt sorry for that horse as I doctored him. He nibbled on the grain a little, but spent more time looking at me while I worked on him than he did eating. He was a tough old booger and never flinched a bit; but every time I'd move, he'd turn his head and follow me with his eyes. He looked at me as if he just couldn't believe that I had ridden him.

When I got through doctoring him, I took him out to the pasture and turned him loose. He walked off slowly for a little ways; then stopped and half turned toward me. He stood there looking at me for several minutes. After a bit, he shook his head up and down slowly and nickered very gently; then he turned and walked on out to a shade tree.

I went back to my cabin, which I'd inherited from Rodriguez, along with the cowboss job.

There in the doorway, with a pitcher of cool lemonade, was Nan waiting for me.

"I guess you know that's the first time Applesauce was ever ridden," she says.

Nodding to her, I told her, "If I have anything to say about it, it'll be the last time anybody'll ever get on him too."

It was like a touch of heaven to sit there in the shade with a cool drink and listen to Nan talk, mostly about Applesauce's life. I was extremely tired, and it was so comfortable, I must have dropped off to sleep. My thoughts were jumbled, with fits of wild bucking horses intermingled with Nan's lovely face; everything confused and mixed up, the way dreams often are. Then it seemed as if she came to me and washed my dirty, sweaty face with a clean, damp cloth. Placing her hands over my eyes, she softly kissed me, and then faded away. After that I slept soundly, for how long I don't know, but when I woke up the sun had moved way across the sky.

Remembering the long battle with Applesauce, I looked down at my dirty, sweaty clothes. I went in my cabin to wash and clean up. There was a little mirror about a foot square hanging there on the wall above my wash pan. As I bent over to get some water, I caught a glance of myself in it; and I froze. There wasn't a bit of dirt or sweat anywhere on my face! I don't know how long I stood there, thinking my thoughts, and remembering my dreams. Or were they dreams? That couldn't really have happened; or could it?

It was a joyous crew that pulled out on the steer roundup that next afternoon. There wasn't a man in the outfit that had any doubts about me being picked as cowboss.

Nanette was riding beside me, and Pop rode out with us for quite a ways. Finally he stopped his horse; so we did likewise. He almost had tears in his eyes as he looked at us and says, "You guys be careful. Have a good gather, and don't worry none about that old horse of yours. I'll take good care of him."

We sat quietly and watched him ride back down the trail; then we turned and galloped to catch up with the rest of the crew.

North Canyon was a good roundup camp. It had cold running spring water, piped into several stock tanks; a water lot, and a large, round pole horse corral. There was about a section fenced in there, which meant we had a pasture to put the remuda in and a holding pasture for our first steer gather.

We got to camp early. We'd planned on butchering a beef for camp meat, but one of the boys had his rifle along and shot a large buck that had come into water at the spring. That fresh venison was a welcome change to most of the crew. I'd lived on it most of the summer, but I never grew tired of it.

The outfit took advantage of a leisurely evening. This would be the last day for a month or more that wasn't cram-packed full of action.

After supper, Nan and I climbed up on a rimrock to watch the sun go down. It was a thrill to be alone with her. There were so many things I wanted to say to her, but I always seemed to lose my nerve. I guess talking to a girl like her was harder for me than riding a horse like Applesauce. I was afraid she'd laugh at me and my cowboy ways; and after the novelty wore off, she'd go back to the city life and her movie career. I couldn't understand her interest in me. I was just another cowboy, but I wasn't about to question it, or miss one little tiny fraction of the enjoyment of being with her; for I knew that any man in the outfit would have died for her without question. As for all the city dudes she knew, she undoubtedly could have her pick of the best, with the crook of her little finger.

I didn't really have time to worry about all that though, for tomorrow, when the work started, it would mean I'd be busy twenty hours a day or more until we were finished.

Sometimes when we were together like up on the rim that night, we'd just sit and enjoy the desert sounds without talking. That evening, we climbed quite high, where we could see miles of country. Nan asked if I could locate where my Lost Canyon was, which I pointed out to her. I had never mentioned the cabin to anyone, for some unknown reason. This evening, I told her about it. She was so thrilled, she wanted me to tell her the whole story; from the day she whispered goodby to me there by the stagecoach until the day she saw me again at the cookshack.

I described the cabin, and told her about everything that happened, except finding the gold. No one knew I had it, which was just as well, I figured.

When Nan asked if I'd take her to see the canyon and the cabin, it brought reality suddenly back to me. Here I was, just a drifter, with nothing to my name but a saddle and a bedroll, talking about wild horses and an old shack full of pack rats; to an educated, wealthy girl who was just beautiful enough to have a promising movie career. The dejected thoughts that rushed in my mind must have shown in my face.

"What's the matter, Red?" she asked, as she put her hand on mine, and looked straight up at me. "Don't you want me to see your canyon?"

Looking at her lovely face, softly pale in the moonlight, it was all I could do to restrain myself. I wanted so much to hold her close and kiss those sweet tantalizing lips, but I was sure any attempt toward a romantic notion on my part would finish me completely with her. She had accepted me for a friend, and that I must remain; for I sure didn't want anything to spoil the wonderfulness of her company for the next month.

It was hard to tell her what I thought; that after a month of dust and dirt, she'd probably be extremely tired of it all. If she stayed for the whole roundup, riding and working hard for eighteen hours a day, she wouldn't be the least bit interested in spending another two or three days riding and camping just to see some old lost canyon.

As I talked, I could see the expression on her face change, and I thought she must be taking my words for a refusal. I finally managed a weak smile, and told her there wasn't anything I would enjoy doing more than to show her my canyon; but by then the movie company would be hounding her, and she would be glad to get back to her friends in town, and to an easier type of life.

She laughed and said, "You silly cowboy, you don't know me very well. I was raised on this ranch astraddle a horse, and I'll never get tired of riding. And that movie career doesn't mean nearly so much to me now as it did awhile back."

She smiled at me again, holding her hand out like a man for a handshake, and said, "I'll make you a bet; that if you're willing to take me to your Lost Canyon after the roundup, that I'll be ready to go."

"I won't bet with you, Nan, but if that's what you want, we'll sure do it," was my delighted answer.

I could have stayed up on those rocks with her forever, but instead, we reluctantly went back to camp and a short night's sleep, before the the month of hard work started.

That first morning was a wild one. Several of the cowboys had brought along, as part of the remuda, some old circle horses that were pretty snorty and cranky. Some of these hadn't been ridden for several months, and they'd just as soon not be ridden again.

We'd long since finished breakfast that morning, when the sun popped over the rim to look down on a cow camp full of activity. Everywhere you looked there was a horse hobbled, with a hind foot tied up. and a cowboy saddling. Three or four of the older cowboys who had gentler horses, had caught and saddled them first, and were helping other boys in dragging their broncs out of the remuda, or were holding them snubbed up while they were being saddled.

I hadn't ridden the two extra horses Tex had cut out for me to bring along. One was a tall rangy thoroughbred-looking black, and the other was a small chunky pinto. The black looked like a circle horse so I caught him that morning. As I was leading him out to my saddle, Tex called to me, "Hey Boss, old Whistler there isn't nearly so gentle as Applesauce was. You better watch him."

His bantering remark was overheard by most of the crew, and was answered by quite a few "Haw, haws," in good nature.

Whistler bowed up and tried to buck a little, but I didn't have time to play games that morning. It didn't take long to knock the buck out of him.

One boy got bucked down that first morning, out of the several that went for bronc rides; but on his second try, he got his horse rode, and we galloped out on our first circle; Nan, Tex, and me leading a pretty good crew of real ranch cowboys.

That day was a forerunner of the next three weeks. A long hard circle, gather cows, work the roundup, cut out the market steers, move them down, grab a quick bite of food, catch a fresh horse, do the same thing over. Fall in your blankets for an exhausted two hours sleep, take your turn at night guard; move camp, horses bucking, running and sometimes falling; long days, short nights; shoeing horses, holding a frightened herd of steers in a sudden desert hailstorm, and a jillion other happenings. It seemed like one long continuous day.

It was hard work, but it was fun. It was man's work, but Nan rode right along with the rest of us, day and night. We were together almost constantly, but seldom alone, or relaxed enough to talk about anything except the work.

Sometimes out on a roundup, the only way you can find time to rest a bit is if you take a fall and get stove up.

One morning, we'd made an exceptionally good gather. We got to the roundup grounds with six or seven hundred head of steers, of all ages and descriptions. There were always a few strays and a few cows that had worked over into the steer range that had to be worked out. An old cow in a steer herd like that can sure cause a lot of problems in a roundup. This day was one of them. Tex and I rode into the roundup herd to cut out the cows and strays first; so we could get them out of the way before we started to classing up the steers.

One old mossy horned cow sure was cantankerous. Two or three times I cut her out of the herd, and she'd make a wild run and get away from someone and dive right back into the middle of the herd. I was riding my pinto horse that day, and was he ever a good one. That old sook never had a chance when we took after her. After the last time she got back into the herd, I decided the next time I cut her out, I'd give her a good chase; then tail her and bust her a good one; and maybe she'd be glad to keep out of our way.

When we came out of the herd, it was in a run, with me whacking her rump with my romal at every jump, until we were traveling about as fast as she could go. Then I rode up beside her, reached down and grabbed her tail in my right hand, throwing my leg over it as I took a couple of turns around the saddle horn, and I rode on by her. Things should have worked out alright; I'd done that same stunt many a time on the range, but this time something went wrong. Just as I raced on by her, that good horse of mine must have caved through a badger den or sage rat den; anyhow his front end just fell right out from under us, and down we went in a pile; horse, cow, and cowboy!

I never had a chance to step out of the way. The boys that were close by said it was hard to tell who was riding what for awhile. Pete, the horse, was going end over end; old Sooky was going end over end; and I was first slammed down in the middle of both of them and then knocked into the air and slammed back down again.

When I quit bouncing and finally stopped, I was sitting up, facing away from the roundup, but behind Pete and old Sooky. I could tell I hadn't broke anything, but I sure felt badly bent; and my face was some scuffed up.

Pete was standing spraddle-legged, facing me with a bewildered look to him, and old Sooky was sliding to a stop on her side, heading away from us. It didn't take her long to scramble to her feet, let out a bawl, throw her tail over her back, and hit a run for open country.

143

She'd had enough cowboying for awhile.

I managed to get up and hobble over to Pete, but I had been slammed hard enough to feel pretty woozy. Tex and Nan came galloping up just as I was trying to climb back on Pete.

Tex took one look at me and says, "Damn, Booger, that was one whale of a tumble. You don't look so good. Maybe you better ride over to the wagon and take it easy for awhile."

I didn't feel like talking or arguing; so I just nodded my head, reined Pete around and headed for camp. As we turned, I swayed and almost toppled off Pete; I didn't seem to have any sense of balance. Nan spurred her horse in beside mine and reached over to steady me. She told Tex she'd ride to camp with me.

It was a good thing the wagon was only about a mile away. I found it a real problem, just trying to stay in the middle of Pete's back. Nan unsaddled and turned him loose for me when we got there. Then she led me over to her teepee and insisted I stretch out on her bed. It sure felt good. It was so much softer and fluffier than what us cowboys' beds were.

I didn't pass out, but I was so dizzy I had to stay real still to keep from falling off her bed, which was rolled out on the teepee floor.

Presently she left and returned with a washpan full of warm water, some medicine, and clean cloths. I pretended to be asleep. She was so gentle and loving as she washed up my skinned, bloody, dirty face; then she doctored it almost like I was a baby that she didn't want to disturb.

It was hard not to open my eyes wide. I had been peeping out from under the corners of the lids, keeping track of her. She finished her doctoring and laid her medicine back on the teepee floor; then bent closely over my face to examine the cuts and scratches again.

I couldn't play possum any longer. When I opened my eyes and smiled at her, I said, "Do you think I'll live Doc?"

"You old meanie. You've been awake all the time," she answered, smiling back at me.

Her face was so close to mine, and she was so pretty. My arms

144

stole up around her of their own accord. It didn't take any force to draw her to me.

That was the first time I kissed her, and it wasn't a one-sided kiss either.

Finally she raised up on her elbows and looked at me, with her eyes shining like stars. A hint of a tear was in the corners, as she whispered to me, "Booger Red, tell me something?"

"What would you like to know?", I smiled at her.

"What you're thinking?," she whispered.

I couldn't keep my feelings to myself any longer. I had to tell her how I felt, regardless of the consequences.

"Nan," I whispered, "I love you so much I can hardly stand it. I have loved you with all my heart and soul, since that first day I saw you, hanging out of that coach window. I don't know what I'll do when you go back to your movie career. I could never live that kind of life."

She silenced me by putting her fingers on my lips. Then, speaking softly, she said, "Red, you needn't worry about that. It was fun for awhile, but I know I could never be happy with that movie life either. As I told you once before, you are the first and only man I've ever been interested in, and that's still true. You red-headed booger, I love you like I never thought I could love anybody. I can hardly bear to be out of your sight."

Then we were in each other's arms again.

I could hardly believe what I'd heard, but stroking her soft hair and holding her close was as close to heaven as I ever hoped to get. All I could think of was how did a wandering cowboy like me ever get this lucky. Then to assure myself that it wasn't just another dream, I'd have to tilt her face toward me and kiss her again.

I was very tired and badly bruised from the fall; but with Nan in my arms, I was so happy and relaxed, that in just a short time, I drifted off into the most peaceful, restful sleep I'd ever known.

I awoke to the sound of approaching horses. Nan was still asleep in my arms.

I raised up on one elbow and could see the day had marched on to evening, from the angle of the shadows. When I looked back at Nan, her green eyes were open and she was smiling.

"Hello you wild desert cowboy," were her words.

"Hello yourself, you cowboy tamer," I teased.

She reached up a hand behind my neck and pulled me to her.

It sure was heck to be interrupted to the sound of crunching cowboy boot heels and jingling spurs.

Then Tex's voice was calling, "Hey, Booger, are you alive?"

I smiled at Nan and whispered to her what I was thinking; then turned and sat up on the bed and answered, "Yeah, Tex, I would be if that grub spoiler would feed me instead of making me wait all afternoon till the crew got in to eat."

Nan poked me right in the sorest spot in my ribs and teased, "You've shore been suffering, haven't you cowboy?"

Then Tex stuck his head in the teepee opening and wanted to know how I felt.

"Well, if I don't starve to death, I think I might be able to ride out in the morning."

Tex laughed and said it looked like I had been pretty well doctored, and that the cook said supper'd be ready in about five minutes.

It hurt some to get up and walk, but the dizziness was gone. With Nan beside me, I got over to the chuckwagon and took on a feed of fresh beef steak, sourdough biscuits, and beans and coffee. After that I really started feeling better.

Nan and I walked out on a ridge away from camp that evening. We sat and talked 'till way late. We had a lot to tell each other, but mostly we just enjoyed being together.

The next morning I rode out on Pete again, since he was my gentlest horse. I was some sore and stiff, but all I needed was exercise to limber up again. I didn't try to tail-bust any cows that day though.

About a week later, we'd finished working the steer range. When we counted the market steers, we had about one hundred head more than what the contract called for. That would give the buyer a chance to go through them and cut back a few if there were any he didn't approve of.

Next morning, we started for the railroad shipping corrals, which were about a week's trail distant. This would give us just about enough time to get there a day ahead of the agreed upon delivery date.

Most of the steers in the trail herd were already pretty well herd broke; so it wasn't much of a chore to line them out on the trail. That was a beautiful sight to my mind, seeing that herd strung out for a couple miles across the desert.

The days were pretty easy, trailing the herd or holding them on grass when we'd come to a good spot. We had to stand guard five nights in a row on the trip.

Nan and I spent a lot of time together. There were some sly remarks made where we could hear them; but I noticed if she came up to where I was working, the cowboys on either side quickly found a job that took them off aways from us, so we could talk privately if we wished.

She wasn't assigned a regular shift on the night guard, but she got up and rode out with me each night on the graveyard shift. Those hours in the dark sure went fast with her sharing the guard with me.

One morning, just as the false dawn started to appear in the eastern sky, the steers became restless and started to moving. There was only Nan and myself and two other cowboys on guard. We couldn't hold the herd, but we were able to get them headed in the right direction. We kept them bunched up and in a fairly close herd. The sun had climbed a long way up across the sky when we finally came to a good valley with grass and water. By then, the steers were willing to stop and graze.

About that time, the crew came galloping over the ridge behind us. Tex apologized for catching up to us so late, but said we must have really moved right along. As soon as the daylight shift of the guard had ridden back into camp and told them we'd already drifted out with the herd, they had all hurried as much as possible. When they saw that we were traveling in the right direction, Tex had sent one of the boys back to the wagon to tell the cook he'd just as well break camp and head on up the trail.

Since the valley we were now in was to have been the end of that full day's drive, and where we'd be camped until we moved on into the shipping pens, Tex said we might just as well wait as the wagon should be along directly.

Town was only about five miles further on. Nan and I decided we'd ride on in and see if Mr. Tom, Pop, and the cattle buyers were there yet.

We figured we wouldn't starve before we got to town, and the idea of eating in a restaurant for a change sounded like an excellent idea. We were hungry, but we didn't want to wait for the wagon. Besides, it would be the first chance we'd had to be alone in days and days.

The past two weeks since my fall had been busy. If it was possible, they'd been longer and harder than before, because as the size of the market herd had increased, so had the amount of work. It was hard to find time to eat, and maybe catch three or four hours sleep out of each twenty-four.

There just hadn't been enough time to do any romancing, but still Nan and I had managed to exchange glances or hold hands; and occasionally even catch a quick kiss. Indeed, it was a thrill to me, just having her near, riding together whenever possible, or sitting side by side while we grabbed a quick meal at the chuckwagon; but there was no chance for serious talking.

That morning when we left the herd in Tex's care and headed for town, the strain of the roundup was almost over. We had the market herd gathered and held just outside of town. Of course, we still had to show them to the buyer, drive them into the shipping pens, and load them on the train; but we felt almost carefree as we rode out of sight of the crew, and gradually slowed our pace.

We had a set of low desert hills to cross over on the way to town. As we neared their crest, a rain shower blowed up fierce and cold. There were some large pinon trees which beckoned to us with their shelter. Nan and I both had slickers tied on the backs of our saddles; so of course, we undid them and put them on. As I did so, I felt something solid in the pocket. It had been quite awhile since I'd had it on, and I'd forgotten what it was. As I drew it out, to our delight, we found it was a little sack of deer jerky which I'd made up while I was in Lost Canyon. We sat down out of the wind, with our backs against the tree trunk and had a snack.

It didn't take long for the old problem to creep up in my mind; what would Nan do now that the roundup was about over? Was she serious about having lost her interest in the movies or would she be anxious to be getting on to Hollywood?

Finally I summoned up enough nerve to broach the subject. In between bites of jerky, and smiling at her lovely but slightly dirty face, I asked her, "Nan, will you tell me something?"

"Uh huh, Booger," she grinned, with her mouth full of jerky, "What would you like to know?"

"Lots of things, my little she cowboy, but mainly right now, how serious are you about not going back to the movies?"

With her hunk of jerky held out in front of her, kind of pointing at me, she became very sincere.

"Booger Red, you are the only thing in the world that truly interests me. The movies are all in the past."

I wrapped my arms around her and kissed her again and again.

"Nan," I whispered, "You are the one I have been hunting for all my life. Will you marry me?"

She drew back and looked up at me, smiling, with a tear in her eye.

"My Booger Red," were her words, "I was beginning to wonder if you would ever ask. Those are the words I have waited for so long. Yes, my darling red-headed cowboy; the sooner, the better!" Then she snuggled close in my arms again, with her head on my shoulder, not exactly sobbing, but softly crying from sheer happiness.

That was a time to remember. We sat there a long time, leaning against a tree, locked in each other's arms, while the wind and the rain lashed down at us; but the fierceness of the elements was nothing compared to the burning love we had for each other.

Finally we drew back where we could look at one another, and I said, "When? A week? A month? Or longer?"

She hushed my talk with her fingers on my lips, and gently spoke.

"As soon as you cowboys get the cattle on the train and can get back to the hotel and get ready. Uncle Tom and Aunt Diana and Pop will all be in town. We can have the wedding there in the church, and then you and I can take our pack trip honeymoon to your Lost Canyon. Our Lost Canyon!"

She looked toward me solemnly for a moment. Then she asked, "Red, can we wait? Can we start our honeymoon after we reach the cabin in the canyon?"

"Nan, dear, it will take us at least two nights on the trail to reach the Canyon. We may have some problems."

"Please Red," was her almost inaudible request.

I drew her closer to me. Looking deep into her beautiful, wistful green eyes, I answered, "Yes, my lovely Nan. It will be awfully difficult, but if that's your wish, that's the way it'll be."

"Oh Nan", was all I could say, as her arms slipped around my neck and we sealed our promise with a wonderful kiss.

The storm blowed over, and the sun came out. We tied our slickers back on our saddles and rode on to town.

Other than the jerky, we hadn't had anything to eat all day; so after we corralled our horses at the stockyards, we stopped at the "Cowboy Inn" and ordered a good meal. Nobody paid any particular attention to us there, as they were used to feeding cowboys just in off the range.

We were just finished eating, when Nan put her hand on my arm. Smiling proudly at me, she said, "I'll tell them Red." She was referring to Mr. Tom and Pop who were just entering the Inn with another man in tow, whom we took to be the cattle buyer. Anyhow we assumed that from his dress and a shirt pocket full of cigars. I answered her request with a nod, as the trio approached our table.

Tom was saying, "Speaking of the devil, aren't you two a ragged looking pair of steer chasers?"

I stood up and stuck out my hand and says, "Hello Tom. Hello Pop."

Tom bent down and embraced Nan and asked her, "How are you, Honey? You kids look like you've had a rough month."

Turning to me, "How do the steers look? Did you get a full count? When will they get in to the holding meadow?"

"About three hours ago," I grinned. "They started drifting on us early this morning. We couldn't stop them so we pointed them in the right direction and were in the meadow by the time our daylight relief caught up with us."

Somewhere along there Mr. Tom had introduced us to the cattle buyer with them. After we all had coffee, he informed me they had left their horses there in the stockyards; so if I felt up to it, he'd see Nan to the hotel where Mrs. Tom was, and then we'd ride out and show the buyer the steers.

Pop, the buyer, and I went on out after the horses.

Mr. Tom seemed to be in a very thoughtful mood when he joined us. I noticed he cast several apprehensive glances in my direction but never mentioned what was on his mind. I could guess!!!

The buyer liked the looks of the steers and rode through them for an hour or more. When he rode back to where we were, he was full of praise of our steers. I was proud when he said he'd only spotted two or three steers in that whole herd that he didn't like. That wasn't even enough to be concerned about, so he wouldn't even make a cut. He'd take the whole herd on a gate count across the scales; so we wouldn't have any extras to worry about.

The full train of cattle cars were due in town that afternoon. We could start loading the next morning as soon as we finished weighing and counting them. Actually he'd lined up a crew to start loading them as fast as they came off the scales.

We trailed the herd on into the stockyards that afternoon. By 11 a.m. the next morning, we had them all weighed, loaded, and on their way. There were one hundred car loads of steers in that special cattle train that morning when it chugged out of the stockyards, heading east. It was a sight that the crew was proud of. We were all there, watching it. Some of us afoot, some ahorseback, and all of us ready to head to the chuckwagon.

Mr. Tom held us up a minute.

"Boys, I'll see you all down at the wagon in a little while with some wages and some real important news. Just as soon as Pop and I, and this cattle buyer, get to the bank and finish our deal."

There were some speculative glances cast their way as they rode off. I tried to act unconcerned as to what the news might be, but I sure had butterflies in my stomach.

The boys were all excited about the statement concerning their wages. Money had been pretty tight for so long that there hadn't been a full payday for a long time. This was the first big cattle sale from the ranch in several years.

We expected our noon meal to be ready when we got back to the wagon, but we were in for a surprise.

When one of the boys asked, "How long till chuck, Cookie?" he received a real dressing down and scolding. The cook informed him that Mr. Tom and Pop were coming out for dinner. Nan had stopped by the wagon that morning and visited with him. She'd told him that and some other things.

It seemed like he gave me a dirty look about that time. I could imagine...

The law was, there wouldn't be one crumb of food set out on the chuck box lid table until the boss got there, and if we went to pestering him, he might stall it off awhile longer.

"You boys remember this, too. Mr. Tom won't pay one cent of wages until we're through eating; so keep out of his way if you want your pay."

We made ourselves scarce around that cook tent. He wasn't really as tough as he pretended, though, for in about fifteen minutes, he sent the horse wrangler out to tell us the coffee was ready, and we could have some if we didn't bother him. As tired and worn out as the whole

152

crew was from the month's work, nobody was taking a nap. I guess they all were thinking about the wages they'd be drawing pretty soon. Some of them had almost a year's wages coming. At $30 or $40 a month, that still amounted to quite a sum.

Most of us filed in and got our coffee; then sat there quietly sipping it, tormenting ourselves with the smell of dinner simmering on the back of the stove.

I decided Nan must have told the cook of our plans. I knew he was one of her trusted friends. He'd slipped her goodies from his kitchen since she could remember.

Every so often he'd look toward me with sort of a dark frown on his face, but he never said a word. I tried to keep him from realizing I was noticing his actions.

When Mr. Tom and Pop returned, they tied their horses at a nearby corral and came right into the cook tent. Mr. Tom was in the lead and was carrying a leather satchel which he set on the chuck box lid. Grinning at the cook, he came out with, "I reckon you still carry that hoglaig of yours along in the chuck box, don't you?"

When the cook nodded, "Yes," he continued.

"Well, don't let any of these ornery cowboys get their hands on it or the rest of us'll get together and crucify us a cook."

Everybody had a good laugh.

We had a good meal of beefsteak and all the trimmings that day. It wasn't a hurry-up race like most of our chuckwagon meals had been for the last month.

Pop and Mr. Tom were in good humor and ate slow and talked a lot and visited with all the boys. I sort of sat over out of the way and didn't take part in much of the conversation.

Finally after much coffee, Mr. Tom asked the cook to bring his satchel to him. He opened it and took out a dog-eared notebook and thumbed through it for awhile. When he found what he was looking for, it was a page with each cowboy's name in one column and the wages he had coming in another. He passed the satchel to Pop. As Mr. Tom called each man and the amount due, if there were no objections,

Pop counted out the greenbacks and handed them over.

Since I was the last man to be hired, I was the last name on the list to be called.

Mr. Tom had asked all the cowboys to wait until he was through paying everybody before anyone left.

The crew was setting around drinking coffee and smoking Bull Durham when Mr. Tom finished his bookkeeping, put the notebook back in the satchel and once again handed it over to the cook for safekeeping.

He then got up, stretched, and walked out into the midst of the crew and got real serious again.

"Boys, I said there'd be some news to tell you and there is. First off, we'll all take some time off. This is Wednesday. You can all have the rest of the week until Monday morning off. But be back here ready to move the wagon back to the ranch Monday morning."

"Now, we might have some special reason for a grand fiesta celebration here in town. A lot of that depends on Booger Red."

If Mr. Tom didn't have the crew's attention before, he did now. Everybody was trying to figure what I'd have to do with their celebrating.

"You all see, that son of a gun has stolen our little Nan's heart, and they are planning on getting married right here in town tomorrow afternoon."

I could feel my face heating up as all eyes turned toward me, when that bombshell was dropped. Nobody said a word.

Mr. Tom continued, "I haven't said yes or no yet. You all know how much she means to Diana and me. Some of you know the story. How she was my brother's only child, and how they came by the ranch when she was a small girl and left her with us when they went on a trip to the east. And how they were killed in a car wreck a few days later. Diana and I never had any kids; so we raised Nan like she was our own."

"It's hard to give away your daughter. I haven't said anything to Red yet, though I'd like to, but I understand Tex had a little chat with him, and that Booger talked right back."

This brought a laugh from the crew.

Then Mr. Tom went on.

"I've decided I'll make up my mind and give my answer when Red walks up to me and asks for Nan. That is, with one stipulation. I know how all you boys are going to hate to lose her to Red also; so if you boys'll form two lines facing each other, two chap lines, I'll get at the far end. Then we'll see if that little girl-stealer dares to come ask me for her."

Then Mr. Tom walked out a ways and turned, facing the cook tent.

Slowly and solemnly the crew got up and walked out to form the lines. Some of them had belts in their hands, some had quirts, some had leather straps, and the rest had their chaps.

I didn't know if Mr. Tom hated me or not, but one thing for sure; he was serious.

Everybody was in place. Still not a word was spoken. They were waiting on me.

"Damn."

I stood up slowly and slipped out of my faded Levi jacket, and then stepped out in the middle of the line. How I wanted to break and run and get it over in a hurry, or to turn and bolt to the side. I could see all the crew cocked and primed. Their quirts and belts ready and hatred in their eyes. Just waiting for me to step past them.

The muscles in my back were tight and burning as I stepped between the first two men, and I clenched my teeth to ward off the slashes. I couldn't let on like I felt a thing.

I was past the first two boys, but nothing had happened. Had I steeled myself so I couldn't feel the pain? I walked that full line and never felt a blow; for not a man lifted a hand against me!

When I got to the end, Mr. Tom was holding out his hand. With a tear in his eye, he was saying to me, "Welcome to the family, Booger Red."

Then all the crew was swarming around, patting me on the back and congratulating me on my luck to be the one to win Nan. What a celebration they were planning.....

Cowboys enjoy playing tricks on each other, more than any group of people anywhere else possibly could. This day, they had played the granddaddy of them all on me, I was sure. It was some time later that I learned that Mr. Tom had passed the word out to the crew they were going to run me through the "Chap Line" for a joke on me. He did save the "why" to the last minute.

Chapter VIII

WEDDING BELLS

It doesn't take much in a western ranch community to cause the entire population to turn out for a celebration. Everybody in that corner of the state seemed to know Nanette, and I think they all came to the wedding.

We were married in the little community church by the local preacher. The church was filled to overflowing, clear out to the street. Diana had commissioned the local bakery to make a large wedding cake. They had planned the reception to be held in the church, but since so many people had shown up, and since it was such a nice day, it was held in the city park band pavilion which was just across the street.

It was a great day, and I could hardly believe that Nan and I were really married. The cake had been cut, refreshments served, and the presents opened. Then it was time for Nan and me to leave.

Nan held me to the promise to take her to the Lost Canyon. We could have driven somewhere in an automobile first, but Nan wanted to spend our honeymoon in the Lost Canyon.

Tex had our saddle horses and a pack horse loaded and ready. We climbed out of our wedding clothes and into new cowboy clothes, and rode out on the trail just as a full moon was climbing up out of the desert floor.

I hated to see Nan take her wedding gown off. She had been so beautiful in that full, floor-length gown with white flower embroidered satin and lace.

I gave Nan several gifts that night, but the one she cherished the most was a small box with two of my gold coins in it, with a note inside. The note read:

Dearest Nan,
Here are two coins which I will make into a necklace
for you. I would have done it before, but I just
haven't had the time.

All my Love,
"Red"

I made the necklace while we were honeymooning in the Canyon. One of the coins I pounded into a long wire, which I then fashioned into chain links. The other coin was used as the pendulum."

"Annabelle, that is the necklace that you have in your jewelry case. Now you know why I have always been so concerned when I've seen you wear it. It was one of Nan's most prized possessions, and is one of the few things of hers that remained to me after she was gone. Later on, I'll tell you how you came to have it."

"One of the most prized gifts Nan gave me that day was this old .45 caliber revolver that I still have. Her note said it was to replace the one I lost that day up on the mesa, chasing the stagecoach. It was brand new when she gave it to me.

We had a whale of a send-off that night. We thought we'd just slip out and ride off into the night without anyone knowing what our plans were, but Tex, our tried and true friend, casually let it slip out. Half the cowboys in the country rode out of the dark and surrounded us, and took us right back down Main Street and on through town. Every man there had at least one pistol on. You would have thought it was the 4th of July, and Pancho Villa had just raided a border town, what with all the shooting and shouting and carrying on. More than one street light clattered to the dust that night. Mr. Tom said afterward, the town presented him with a bill of over $200.00 for damages, and replacing lights that were shot out that night.

We finally pulled up out at the edge of town. We made a little thank you speech to the boys, and I persuaded them we'd been chivareed and escorted far enough. They all wished us well, and sat and watched as we rode off into the night.

We rode most of the night. It was such a beautiful night, and we were too excited to be tired.

It was almost the false dawn of the morning, when we came to a boxed in spring that had a small meadow below it with good grass for our horses.

After stripping off their gear, we hobbled them, and then rolled our one bedroll out. The night had suddenly become quite chilly; so we pulled our boots off and crawled under the blankets to cuddle in each other's arms.

We talked of what a wonderful day it had been, and how nice it would be when we reached the sanctuary of the cabin in the Lost Canyon. The promise I'd made to her that day in the rain, to wait until we reached the cabin to start our honeymoon, was fresh in my mind; so I just held her gently, and sleep soon claimed both of us.

We spent one more night camping on the trail; then late in the afternoon of the second full day, we rode into the canyon and up to our cabin. It was just as I had left it. I stepped to Nan before she dismounted and caught her in my arms. Kissing her, I carried her across the small porch. It was some difficult getting the latch unfastened and the door opened with one hand; but I managed, and then carried her across the threshold. I stood her gently on the floor and kissed her again. Kidding her, I said, "There Mrs. MacIntosh, you are delivered safely to your castle."

Her arms went around my neck as she drew me to her, laughing, "My King!"

The horses we'd ridden were gentle. After we unsaddled, I took them back down to the spring and shut them up in the water lot. I wanted them to get used to watering there before being turned out in the canyon. We had brought with us all the provisions we needed to stock the camp, as well as a few extra things of Nan's; so we planned to turn the horses out while we were there. Besides, they couldn't get away, since we'd shut the slip pole gate when we'd entered the canyon, so we were sure we could catch them.

We fixed our first supper in the cabin. After I helped her clean up the dishes, I told her I was going back down to the spring to let the horses loose. She told me to go ahead, and not to hurry; that there were some things she wanted to do.

When I returned to the cabin, the day was almost gone. There was a faint glow like the light of a candle coming out the front door. I stepped up to the cabin and called softly, "Nan, may I come in?"

"In a minute."

Then I heard her moving and the barest whisper, "Red."

There, in the open doorway, she stood like an angel, a vision in white! So beautiful, I just stood there amazed, afraid to move. Unknown to me, Nan had carefully rolled her wedding dress up that night and had brought it along. Now she stood there before me. My bride; smiling and blushing, holding her hands out gently toward me. Instantly I was beside her, and our embrace was one I have remembered all my life.

As I blew out the candle, I whispered softly to her.

"I, Daniel, take thee, Nanette, to be my lawful wedded wife. Nanette, my darling wife."

What a wonderful week we spent there. Nan was so loving and warm. Each day I managed to find a few wild flowers to bring her. We explored the canyon, finding many new hidden nooks I hadn't seen before. We worked some on the cabin. Nan made some curtains for the two small windows, and added other feminine touches, bringing warmth and life and love, changing the small cabin from a house to a home. Also, I finished Nan's necklace that week.

We hated to leave at the end of a week, but we'd promised Tom and Diana we'd see them in about ten days. Besides, we were about to run out of grub, so finally we had to catch up the horses and head out. I have never been back to the Canyon since.

We camped one night on the way back and rode on into the ranch in the middle of the second morning. The crew was out working, but Tom and Diana were sitting on the front porch watching for us.

Tom and Diana loved Nan so. Their whole life lit up when she was around. When it finally dawned on them that my marrying Nan would keep her there on the ranch in place of chasing a Hollywood dream, they quickly accepted me. I kept their little girl home.

There was a small but lovely guest house there at the headquarters close to Tom's house which Nan and I moved into. I didn't have to go back to work as the cowboss for another week yet.

They held a welcoming home party for us there at the "Big House" that night. It was really something!

Tom had a law on the ranch against drinking. He wasn't a teetotaler, and he didn't expect his men not to drink; but he wouldn't allow anyone to lay around the ranch tanked up either.

That night the barrier was broken, though. There was a feast set out on tables in the yard that would feed an army, and there were just about that many people there. Ranchers, cowboys, and town folks, and of course, all of the crew were invited.

Tom had hired a good Mexican orchestra that played, starting early in the afternoon. They played through the meal, and then after the tables were cleared from the patio, the affair turned into an all night dance.

I hated to surrender Nan to all those people, but one after another came and claimed the privilege of dancing with her. Finally at the close of a dance after midnight, Nan and I made our way up to the bandstand, where Nan thanked all the people for coming. Then during an intermission, we slipped away from the crowd. We knew better than to go to our house, for we would surely be chivareed some more before morning, if those cowboys knew where we were. We went by my old cabin and got the bedroll we'd used on our honeymoon, carried it to a secluded spot, and spent the rest of a short but wonderful night.

Many of the party-goers had breakfast with us the next morning. There wasn't much work done that day.

Our little house had served as a "powder room" for the gals that night and was in somewhat of a mess. Nan wanted to rearrange it on her own, so I got lost.

Applesauce stood there with his head cocked around to the side, watching me for a minute; then straightened out and slightly arching his neck, raised his head in the air.

I fooled around for awhile, but it wasn't long before I wound up down at Pop's milk cow pasture where old Applesauce was. He was standing in the shade, switching flies, and tried to let on like he didn't notice me; so I sat down on a rock a few feet away from him and just watched him.

Most of his cuts and spur marks were all healed up. He was a beautiful, well-built horse. It was a shame he'd been spoiled when he was young and never been really broke to ride.

After a bit, I became drowsy, so I hunkered down on the ground and leaned back against the rock and dozed off. Presently, hearing a movement, I woke up enough to open one eye partway. There was Applesauce with his ears cocked forward, slowly walking toward me. He came up softly, close enough to be able to sniff at me, which he did from my boots clear to my hat. Then he just stood there and looked at me with ears still pointing ahead.

I raised up a hand to his nose and softly said, "Hello, Old Timer, how're you doin'?"

He sniffed my hand, then gently shook his nose up and down. I stood up then and talking softly to him, ran my hand over his body, examining all the scratches and marks.

Finally with my hand on his head up between his eyes, I gave him one last caress and told him to take it easy. Then I turned and started back to the house. I had just taken a few steps when I was stopped by a soft nicker behind me. When I turned, Applesauce was still standing where I'd left him. With another soft nicker, he shook his nose up and down and seemed to be calling me back to him.

I walked back and stopped at his head. He took a step forward, which put me at his withers. Swinging his nose around, he nudged me gently in the ribs.

Sometimes it is better to act than to think. That's what I did then, by hanging my arm across his withers, jumping across his back, then swinging up in position with a leg on each side. Applesauce stood there with his head cocked around to the side watching me for a minute, then straightened out, and slightly arching his neck, raised his head in the air. Then he started forward in an easy springy walk, right over to the gate, out of the pasture, where I had been headed.

I sat on his back and talked to him, and scratched his neck for a long time before I got off. He nuzzled me gently with his nose, then turned and walked back out in the pasture a ways. He stopped and turned toward me and shook his head in the air again. He seemed to say to me, "We're friends now, so take care of yourself."

There were very few times after that, that I didn't pay him a visit when I came in after being out on the range working.

The fall sailed on.

Life was so wonderful, spending it with Nan. We spent most of our time together. She rode with me almost every day. I helped her do the dishes in the evenings, when we had supper in our house. Of course, we ate quite often in the cookshack with the crew, after spending a long hard day out riding. Many of the suppers and evenings were spent over with Tom and Diana too, so it was really a thrill for the occasional meal we had alone in our house.

Thanksgiving was suddenly there before we even had time to think about it. The ranch cook, Diana, and Nan spent a week, it seemed, cooking pies and goodies for the occasion. The whole ranch crew, Tom, Diana, Nan and I, and many friends and neighbors, all had dinner there together at one long table. I can still see the heaps and heaps of food set out that day; so different from practically every Thanksgiving before in my life. It certainly was a grand occasion.

The time between Thanksgiving and Christmas just seemed to melt away.

The holidays had taken on a new meaning for me. Something I had never known before. This was the first Christmas in my life, since I was a small boy in the orphanage, that I hadn't been alone or out in some God-forsaken line camp; too broke or busy to know what the meaning of Christmas really was.

The festive season really got off to a good start a few days before Christmas actually got there. Somewhere about the middle of the month, the crew and I trailed a herd of steers out to the North Canyon steer range. Nan decided to stay at the ranch as she had many things to do to get ready for Christmas. It was very difficult to ride out and leave her at the ranch. We'd be gone at least three days and two nights. There was no way I could get back any sooner.

The second morning when we saddled up and started out, one of the boy's horses blew up in a wild fit of bucking. This was a normal occurrence, but that morning, he had a little bad luck. When his pony stepped in a soft spot, he fell down and pitched over on him in a rock pile. The boy came out of the deal with a broken arm.

Work doesn't stop with a trail herd when somebody gets disabled; the rest of the crew continues on shorthanded.

It was quite a ways back to the ranch; but there was a 2 Bar camp just over the mountain where a married cowboy lived who had an old car.

Joe Slone was the cowboy with the broken arm. After we got the arm bound up some, he said he could ride over to Rex's camp; so I sent Tex and the crew on with the steers, and I started out with Joe. It was a slow painful ride for him, but he was tough and didn't complain.

Rex was shoeing a horse when we got to his camp. It didn't take long to put up our horses, pile into his old Model A, and head for town.

We had Joe into the doctor's office and bedded down, and his arm worked on by the middle of the afternoon. It was a fairly bad break, and the doctor wanted to keep Joe there for a couple days so as to keep an eye on him. He was pretty worn out, and didn't argue much after I promised to come back to town to pick him up later on.

Rex and his wife and I went to a restaurant then and had our noon meal, which we hadn't been able to have at noon. From four A.M. until four P.M. can sure give a cowboy an appetite.

I couldn't catch up with the crew in time to help them any; so I decided to have Rex drive me back to the 2 Bar. Rex said he had planned on riding over to headquarters in a few days, and he would bring our horses and saddles over when he came.

It was getting late when we got there. I talked Rex and his wife into putting up at one of the extra cabins for the rest of the night. We hadn't aroused any attention from anyone. The house Nan and I had was dark, but there was a light on in Tom's house; so I went up there.

As I approached the house, I could hear music. Someone was playing the piano. I was able to let myself into the parlor without interrupting the playing. There was Nan at the piano, softly singing and playing. Here we'd been married almost four months, and I didn't even know she played the piano. We loved each other so much, but still had a lot to learn about each other.

Totally unaware of me, she was so beautiful that I was spellbound. I stood at the door and listened for quite awhile. She was singing "Danny Boy", and the words of the song brought up a memory from my childhood I hardly knew existed. I must have been only about three years old. My mother was holding me in her arms and she was singing "Danny Boy" to me. That had been somewhere around twenty years ago.

The story of my early life flickered through my mind. Part of it I remembered vaguely, and part was handed down to me in the orphanage.

My parents had homesteaded out near Lake, Oregon, close to Buffalo Wells. Things must have gotten tough because my father went off to work somewhere. He was never heard from again. One day a traveler stopped by our house and found my mother sick, and I was almost starved. By the time help was summoned, my mother was dead. I was sent to an orphanage.

The song was so sad, yet so lovely; there was no way I could interrupt. I reached down and silently unbuckled the spurs from my bootheels; then stole quietly across the room and stood behind Nan with my hat in my hands. She finished her song; then bowed her head and clasped her hands in her lap. The room was completely still. I hadn't made a sound, but somehow our minds were communicating. I guess my Scotch-Irish heritage was calling out to hers.

Presently Nan raised her head and spoke softly.

"My darling Red, I know that's you here in the room with me. That song was to be a surprise for you on Christmas Day Mister Daniel Lewellyn MacIntosh."

I stepped forward then, and bending over, kissed her gently on the neck. Hugging her, I said, "My beautiful, darling, loving wife, I am sorry to have come in at the wrong time, but I have missed you so. It seems I have been gone a month instead of two days. I couldn't interrupt you, and you can play it for me again on Christmas Day and every day thereafter."

Christmas that year was really something special. Nan had told me sometime around Thanksgiving that we would have a baby next year. All the extra plans we made for you, Annabelle, and presents like I had never seen, made me realize how much I had missed.

It was so wonderful, being with Nan, and a part of her family. We all had a big dinner together, everyone on the whole ranch. That was the only Christmas we had together.

Later that night, Nan and I took a bucket of grain down to my old pet, Applesauce.

On Valentine's day, I surprised Nan with a large heart-shaped box of candy. She surprised me with a new white hat, made by Valentine Hat Company out California way.

As spring drew nearer and Nan became heavier, it became very hard for me to get out and do my range work. Tex was a real true friend and shouldered much of my load.

Tom and Diana had finally convinced Nan and me that we should move to town at least a week before you were due, Annabelle. We got all packed and prepared to make the trip to town when Nan started having pains. She said she was afraid we'd waited one week too long. We piled into Tom's big Buick car and roared off for town. That was the longest trip of my life. I was sure we weren't going to make it in time, and every time Nan would have a cramp, I'd get more worried, nervous, and fretful. However, you didn't arrive for eight hours after we got to the hospital, but that was the hardest day I had ever spent in my life at that time. I was completely worn to a frazzle by the time you got there.

169

Tom and Diana tried to let on like it didn't excite them at all. This was all just normal proceedings, and they knew everything would be alright; but I know they were just as concerned as I was, and were just as proud when we finally got to see you. You were their granddaughter just as much as if Nan had been their own child.

It was quite a homecoming when we brought you back to the ranch. Every rancher, cowboy, and Mexican in that corner of the state had to come by to see "the Little Nan."

I was so proud I felt I'd bust. I just had to have somebody to tell all about you, and I thought about Sandy and Monte. They had given me an address up in Montana, and I had promised to write them. That had been almost two years ago when we had parted company up in the Jackson Hole country. In all that time I hadn't written them. Now seemed like the right time.

It was a difficult task, but I sat down and wrote, telling them much of what had happened, and of course, about my new foal. I even sent along a picture.

A couple weeks later, much to my surprise, a letter came to me, postmarked Dillon, Montana. It was a book-length letter from Sandy and Monte. In it, they told of having a son almost a year old. They named him "Danny" after me, and also sent his picture. I was almost as proud of that as I was of you, Annabelle.

Their letter went on to tell that Monte's father had died from injuries he'd received in a fall on a horse. They were taking over the ranch, but things sure were tough, what with all the hospital and funeral bills.

They mentioned several times how they missed me and would like to see me again. They ended their letter by insisting I should come to visit them and bring my family for them to meet. After all, we were almost like relatives.

The bad news in their letter really got to me; to think of Monte and Sandy having really tough times. I still had all that gold I'd found over in Lost Canyon. Maybe I could figure out a way to give them a hand, and branch out a little on my own.

As the Arizona weather really warmed up, I kept thinking about Montana. It sure seemed like it would be a good time to spend a summer vacation up north. When I asked Nan if she'd like to go to Montana to visit my old friends, she was thrilled with the idea.

Tom and Diana told us they sure hated to see us go, but they thought we should. They even insisted we take the big Buick car. They told us to stay all summer if we wanted to.

That day when we left the ranch was the last time I ever saw Tom and Diana. I can still see them standing there, arm in arm, with tears in their eyes as they waved goodby to us. They loved Nan and the baby so much, and had even learned to sort of be proud of me.

Pop was there too, all choked up, not saying a word.

Those people were the salt of the earth.

It was a good trip. We didn't drive fast, but traveled right along. On the afternoon of the fourth day, we drove into the ranch, unannounced.

A cowboy on a bay horse, and a cowgirl on a big buckskin horse were pushing a little bunch of cows and unbranded calves into a corral out along the road. They saw us drive up and stop, but didn't recognize us. I didn't say anything, just sat there watching them, and tingling all over. I could hardly keep the grin off my face.

Finally the gal on the buckskin rode over as I got out of the car. She wanted to know if there was anything she could do for me before she really looked at me. I'm sure old Buck recognized me. Before I could come out with any kind of a wise answer, Monte's face lit up. She was off that horse and in my arms, hugging me all over like a long lost brother.

It didn't take Sandy long then to connect that Arizona license plate on the car and come on at a hard gallop. Sliding to a gravel-kicking stop, he bounded out of the saddle and grabbed me around the neck. That was some reunion.

We had a joyous afternoon that day. Sandy and Monte had been fixing to brand that little bunch of calves, but since we arrived, they wanted to turn them loose. I insisted we pitch in and help brand the calves first, because we were going to stay plenty long enough to get caught up on our visiting before we left.

Old Buck remembered me for sure. There at the car, he came right up to me and sniffed me over and looked me up and down. Sandy couldn't get over it. He kept saying, "Look at that old son of a gun. Damned if he don't remember you. You know that old booger won't hardly let me up to him, even after I been feeding and caring for him for two years?"

We all had a good laugh at Sandy's expense.

Nan was thrilled with my Montana friends, and immediately made up to their little boy. Likewise Monte and Sandy couldn't get over my wife and daughter. They kept wanting to know how I'd been so lucky to find such a wonderful gal.

Late that night after supper, we were setting out watching the beautiful evening sky. Monte happened to think to ask me how my Blizzard horse was. When I replied I'd lost him, they had to know why and how. I told part of the story about running him across the desert and hitting a hidden rock pile where he broke a leg. Nan then told the rest of the story. Why I was running my horse — to save her from a terrible fate in a driverless runaway stagecoach. We were all quiet then for quite some time. It was a time for meditation as we sat there close together.

We had a good time there with Sandy and Monte. Her mother lived there on the ranch with them. When she saw you, Annabelle, she simply adored you. That gave Nan a chance to get out and ride with Sandy, Monte, and me. In a few days, we had all his range work caught up and it was time to start haying. We rounded up his work horses and started working them on the wagons to get the kinks ironed out of them before we hooked them up to the mowers and rakes. We spent close to a month working long hard days in the hay fields.

We'd hook up four mowing machines and all of us mow until the first cut was ready to rake. Then Monte and Nan would ride and buckrake until they caught up with Sandy and me.

It didn't hurt the hay to set in the big buckrake bunches to settle and cure out for awhile; so instead of stacking it right away, we kept right on cutting and raking until we got all the hay down and bunched.

When we started stacking, Sandy and I would switch off with one of us on the stack in the morning and the other in the afternoon. We had good weather, and in a month, we had a lot of sweet wild hay in big stacks all over the meadow.

I hadn't pried into Sandy's and Monte's ranching affairs, but it was easy to see they were pretty hard up. They just had a handful of cows on that beautiful big, thousand head ranch. By the time we were through haying, with what little they had told us, it was plain to see what kind of a predicament they were in. They had to sell most of the cows, and borrow money against the ranch to pay the hospital bills.

The day we finished stacking the last of the hay, we got through a little earlier than usual. Nan and I talked Sandy and Monte into going to town with us and celebrating by having our evening meal in a restaurant. After supper, we were relaxing, sipping on a beer, and trying to figure out how much hay we'd gotten stacked.

In a little while Sandy became morose, and finally said, "Hell, there's no need to try to count up how much hay we've put up. There's ten times more stacked than what our measly little herd of cows will need for the winter, and the chances of selling any around here are pretty slim. Everybody else is almost as poor as we are, or else they also just put up their own hay."

We all sat there quiet awhile until I finally asked Sandy if he figured he had enough ranch and feed to winter a thousand head of yearlings.

"It sure ought to," was his answer. "Monte's dad ran almost that many cows here for years."

173

As I started to talk, I held a very attentive group of people. I outlined a plan that I'd had in mind for some time.

"Sandy," I said, "I've got enough money to stock your ranch with Mexican cattle, and I know where to get them down in old Mexico. I won't say right now how I came to have the money, but it's legal and legally mine, and clean as far as I know. I can deliver the cattle here, clear, and probably come up with enough operating capital to hold over until we have some income from the cattle. I figure if we get five hundred steers and that many heifers, then when the time comes, we'd ship the steers to market and keep the heifers for replacement cattle."

"I'll furnish the cattle and operating expenses. You furnish the ranch and take care of them. You take sixty percent, and I'll take forty percent of the sales. On top of that, you can reinvest my forty percent into cattle or range land until we get built up to a good operation or whatever."

Sandy was so spellbound he couldn't even answer me. I finally had to ask him what he thought of the idea. Then he responded with, "Why Pard, I think that's the best damn news we've heard in a coon's age."

"O.K. then, it's a deal."

We shook hands and started right in to making plans.

We needed to get the Mexican cattle brought up north as soon as possible before the fall and cold weather set in; so they could get used to the change easier.

Nan and I would go to Mexico and make arrangements for the cattle. Sandy would round up about three good Montana cowboys and be waiting to hear from me. As soon as I could, I'd telegraph him where to come to, to pick up the cattle.

It'd take at least two weeks to round up the cattle and trail them across the border to the railroad.

We were all excited and still making plans that night when we got back to the ranch. Monte's mother was still up, and she became as excited as the rest of us when she learned our plans. She came up with a plan that was hard to accept, but it helped solve our problem, and we finally agreed to it.

"You were just a tiny baby, Annabelle. For some reason not clear to me, Nan couldn't nurse you, so you were a 'bottle baby'. Grandma Cook said to leave you and little Danny with her; then we all could concentrate on the cattle. Also, that way, we'd be sure to have an excuse to accompany the herd all the way back up to Montana.

"As hard as it was to go off and leave you there, it still was a good plan at the time, or so we thought. When we left Grandma Cook in charge of you, jokingly we said, "Well, if we don't come back, it looks like you've got another daughter to raise."

The next day we left; Nan with tears in her eyes and me with a lump in my throat. We headed for the railroad and the journey to old Mexico.

We went to Portland, then caught the daylight train for sunny California. Approximately thirty-six hours or so later, we were in Tucson where we rented a car, and were heading south. We had left our car (Tom's Buick), with Sandy, to pick up when we returned.

The Mexican roads weren't very good, and it took quite awhile to make it on down to Hernandez' rancho. I was some apprehensive about meeting them because of my Mexican girlfriend, Lolita. Later on I was relieved to learn that she also was married now, and had a baby of her own.

I was able to make a good deal on the yearlings, and I pleased Senor Hernandez when I agreed to pay an additional fifty cents a head if his crew would help deliver the herd across the border and to the railroad.

Nan and I drove all night that night, to the closest telegraph station to wire word to Sandy to come on, and where to meet us. We waited for his return wire. When it got there the next day stating they were well on their way, we headed back up to Nogales, to meet them when they rolled in. We had a night on the town, followed by a good rest. Then Sandy, Monte, and three wild Montana cowboys stepped off the train.

We had a hard time getting those Montana cowboys out of town that evening. Every time one of those pretty dark eyed senoritas would look their way, they'd go to snorting like a wild prairie mustang and try to break away.

We finally got the crew fed and watered out, and loaded into our car with all their saddles, and headed south. With seven of us in it, that car was loaded down.

While we were in town, I'd made arrangements with the border officials to cross our cattle. I'd also put in an order for enough railroad stock cars to be on hand to ship them north. Things were progressing nicely.

Sandy and his crew were well pleased and surprised when they saw the cattle. They had heard so many stories about the Mexican cattle all being slabsided, ewe-necked, big headed and long horned, that they were unprepared when they were shown a herd of good quality mixed Hereford cattle.

In a few days we had the herd out, shaped up, and headed north for the railroad.

Nan and I decided to leave the car at the ranch so we could ride with the herd. We could come back and get it, return it to Tucson, and then catch the herd on the railroad, before they got clear up to Montana, as the cattle would have to be unloaded for feed and water somewhere along the way.

It took a week to trail to the railroad. It was a good trip even though we had to stand guard every night and didn't get much sleep. It was sort of like that first month Nan and I had spent together on the roundup, only much better since we were married.

It took a couple days to get everything straightened out at the border. Then we turned all our borrowed horses over to Hernandez' crew.

I had been thinking about some ancient Indian ruins I'd found in the mountains long ago which I wanted to show Nan; so I told Sandy if we didn't catch up right away, it would be because we'd decided to take off a week to see them.

Then it was "Goodbye" to Sandy and Monte, as they and their crew pulled out with the trainload of cattle. Nan and I climbed into Senor Hernandez' big Packard and headed back to the rancho to get our rented car.

It's a real thrill to take a ride down across Mexico in such a car with a fiery young Mexican at the wheel. A few times I wondered whether or not we'd get there, but presently we rolled into the ranch. I must say, it took at least two hours less than when Nan and I had driven it down. What a relief it was to get out of that Packard that day.

We decided to skip the pack trip to the mountains and head north right away instead. However Senor Hernandez wouldn't hear of our leaving that day. We had to stay at least overnight for a small fiesta he had planned in our honor.

Chapter IX

OUTLAWS

It doesn't take much of an excuse for those Mexicans to have a fiesta, and when an event occurs like what had just happened to them they really put one on. That cattle sale had been the first sizable amount of cash inflow they'd seen in a long time. Then when I'd paid in good American gold coins—that was something else!

It was way late that night before Nan and I had a chance to slip away from the party. Even though we were dead tired, we decided we'd just get our car and head north instead of going to bed. Otherwise it would be way late tomorrow before we could get away.

I knew the road forked up country a few miles, and that the left hand fork ran up into a high valley where there was running water and a good place to camp. That would be a good place to sleep for two or three hours; then we could get on our way again. When we got there, we were so tired we just stretched out in the car and passed out.

I was having horrible dreams of being surrounded by Mexican bandits. I kept trying to get my .45 out from under the seat, but each time I tried, I couldn't reach it. Then suddenly the dreams became reality as a hard jabbing in the ribs got through to my tired brain and brought me upright.

I remembered thinking that we'd rolled the windows up and locked the doors before we went to sleep, but something was wrong. Very wrong! Something had kept one door from locking, and it was now open. A big Mexican was leaning in the car with a rifle, and jabbing me in the ribs.

"Wake up, Gringo. And if you touch that .45, I'll blow you to pieces."

I had sure been caught off guard. Tired as I was, I guess we should have stayed at the ranch. It was plain to see we were in one hell of a predicament!

The Mex prodded me again.

"O.K. Gringo, wake up the Senora and get out of the car."

It took Nan a few minutes to get wide awake to realize what was happening to us. I could see she was shaken up, but she never let on that she was the least bit frightened.

There were several Mexicans in the group, but it appeared the one ordering us around was a sort of lieutenant, not the leader.

After we got out of the car, the Mexicans ransacked it and took what they wanted of our stuff.

They would have gotten Nan's gold necklace, but for one thing. That night when we stopped, she took it off, saying she was afraid she might break it in the car, and she handed it to me to put up for the night. I had just taken my billfold out of my hip pocket so as not to lose it, so I put the necklace in it. Then I stuck it inside my left boot top. When the Mexicans searched me, they didn't think to check the insides of my boot tops.

After they'd made a mess of the car, they brought one dismounted rider's horse over. I was ordered onto it. The Mexes made Nan get on behind; then we started out toward the high rough back country. The dismounted bandit drove off in our car.

At that time, I think we were still too tired and sleepy to be real worried. We just rode on and on, strung out with that bandit group.

Late that night, the bandits pulled up and pitched camp and started cooking a meal.

Nan and I were staked out to a mesquite tree. That's when I really started to get worried.

The leader of the bandits had stayed away from us all day. I never got a close look at him, but there was something about him at a distance that seemed familiar to me. I couldn't place him though. He was bearded and kept his eyes shaded under his sombrero.

When the supper was ready, the bandit chief filled two plates and brought them to us. As he neared us, he spoke, calling me "Booger Red". Then I knew who it was.

He went on, saying, "I guess you know it's time to pay for all your good fortune. And for stealing my job, and my horses, now don't you?"

"Rodriguez, you greasy coward!"

My answer was cut off by him kicking me in the stomach and dumping my plate of food upside down in the sand at my feet.

He set Nan's plate of food down where she could reach it. He was just barely able to jump back out of the way as she kicked the plate full at him.

"You red-headed spitfire! You'll pay for that. It'll cost Tom his ranch now to get you back!"

He then turned and went back to the cookfire and to his beady-eyed comrades. As they wolfed down their food, they made casual remarks and cast wicked glances in our direction.

Nan and I put in a miserable night that night.

We were dead tired, thirsty, and starved. We'd been given some water earlier in the afternoon, but it began to look like that was to be our last, as the bandits had started to bed down for the night.

Finally one old man brought a canteen over and held it cautiously toward Nan. I coaxed her to nod her head yes; so the old bandit then held the canteen to her lips. When she was through, he turned and looked at me for a minute before holding it out toward me. When I nodded for it also, he gave me a few gulps before turning away.

Nan and I talked about Rodriguez and what he had planned. Things sure didn't look good. He was such a lowdown skunk, it was hard to tell what he might decide to do.

It's hard to find a way to rest or sleep with your hands shackled around a tree behind you. I felt so sorry for Nan. I regretted insulting that Mex, Rod, as maybe I could have talked him into making conditions more comfortable for Nan if I hadn't. However, when I mentioned it to Nan, she said, "Red, that damned lowdown, creepy snake! I was so proud of you when you told him what you did!"

The night wore on. I guess I must have dozed off; for the next thing I knew, there was a Mex stirring up the breakfast fire.

Finally the old Mex that had brought us the water the night before, came over with a sawed off shotgun. He unshackled Nan and told her she could go to the toilet if she wanted, but if she didn't come back pretty quick, he'd blow off my head with the shotgun. After Nan returned, he shackled her with her hands in front of her around a tree limb. Then he handed her a couple of tortillas and a piece of meat. Then he turned me loose, but followed me to the brush with his shotgun, with both hammers pulled back.

He made me shackle myself when we returned to camp. I was given a little food then, which I didn't refuse. I figured I'd need all the strength I could get.

After breakfast, camp was broke. The bandits brought their horses up from somewhere. Nan and I were given separate horses that day. Neither horse was the one we'd ridden the day before. The first thing I noticed about our horses was their brands. They wore the 2 Bar. That damn Rodriguez was really trying to rub it in.

We rode hard all day, stopping only for a few minutes at noon to water the horses. Nan and I were each given some water.

About sundown, we rode into a sort of a ranch or permanent camp. There were a couple shacks and some corrals there.

We were again shackled with our hands behind our backs, this time around the post of a "lick log" or very stout hitch rail. The only way we were able to stand it, was due to the fact the chains between the two wrist cuffs were about one and a half feet long. That way, we could stand or sit down with our hands almost at our sides; or we could extend one hand farther behind us and relax the other a bit by pulling it more to the front. Then we could change position. At the best, it was very uncomfortable.

We were again shackled with our hands behind our backs, this time around the posts of a "lick log", or very stout hitch rail.

The bandits built a campfire and cooked supper. The old Mex brought us two plates of food. As he came up to us, he said, "I'm bringing you this food. You can eat or no. I no care. If you kick it on me, I kill you quick."

We stood still while he set the food down close by our feet. It's quite a trick to feed yourself with your hands shackled behind you around a post, but we finally managed.

That night, instead of bedding down after supper, the bandits built up the fire and started to playing cards and drinking tequila.

Most of the night, Rodriguez sat across the fire from us and sipped on a bottle, which he refused to share with any of the other bandits. Occasionally he and some of his outlaws would get into a heated argument. After each drink from his bottle, he'd look directly over towards us. I mentioned it to Nan. She answered, "He's looking directly at me. Each time it just makes my flesh creep. Red, I'm afraid things are going to be bad before tonight's over."

Then for a long while, he stared at me. Finally he came over and stood looking directly at me. After a bit he says, "Well Booger Red, I've known for a long time that we'd met before the 2 Bar. I just figured out where. You were the cowboy in that bar up in New Mexico that night."

He then took another swig from his bottle and returned to his spot over by the campfire.

There were sixteen bandits in the group. Most of them were drinking pretty heavy. All of them were drinking some but three or four who seemed to have been appointed as guards were taking it a little easier on the tequila. All the bandits were heavily armed, but the guards had automatic rifles and one of them even had a sub-machine gun.

From time to time, Rodriguez would get up and pace back and forth. Then he'd stop and look toward Nan. Several times, he and some of the others got into heated arguments. I was really getting worried, as I could hear Nan's name mentioned several times.

Finally, after midnight, another argument between Rod and two of the younger Mexicans resulted in their reaching some kind of an agreement. They all had a drink out of Rod's bottle; then they came around the fire directly toward us. My heart was pounding so hard, it felt like it was about to split my chest wide open. I was straining and pulling on my shackles until I was about to pull my wrists off. I was sure I knew what those filthy Mexes had in mind.

They came right up to Nan. As Rod approached, he was grinning and laughing. He said, "Now my red-headed bitch, you're going to get what you've had coming for a long time."

The other bandits started making grabs for Nan. One of them got too close. It sure did me good when she placed a well-aimed kick with the toe of her shoe right home in his groin. He toppled over backwards moaning and clutching himself in real pain.

If she hadn't been chained, I'm sure Nan could have fought Rod and the other young Mex off, but by this time, some of the others over by the fire had heard and seen the commotion. It whetted their own desires up to the same pitch, and they came over. It didn't take long for several of them to drag her down on the ground and rip off all her clothes, and proceed with their intentions.

"Oh, God!"

It was more than I could bear. I was pulling and straining and kicking and cussing with all my might, but it only added fuel to their fire.

One Mex squatted down waiting his turn, got too close to me. In a flash I drew back a booted foot and kicked with all the pent up force of my hurt and anger. It was twice the strength of a normal man. I can still hear that Mex's neck snapping as my heavy boot caught him alongside of the head. He was left half-necked in a limp pile face down in the dust.

Nan wasn't crying or whimpering. She might have been screaming, but if she was, it was the scream of a she-panther in full battle. Yet those damn Mexes kept mounting her one after the other, with one or two of them hanging onto each of her legs trying to hold her in spread-eagle fashion. She never gave up fighting, until I saw one of them hit her alongside of the head with his fist and knock her out cold. I was almost relieved to realize she was unconscious and no longer aware of the embarrassment and pain.

I don't know how long all this went on. Most of the bandits had already had their try at her and were laying around asleep or drinking on their bottles. Rodriguez was over by the fire, passed out.

The three guards that were still partly sober came over and took their turns while Nan was still unconscious. With all my shouting and kicking and cussing, I couldn't do anything to stop them.

About this time, one of the bandits brought a big German police dog up on a leash. He was rattling off a bunch of Mex and talking about now they were going to have some real fun to watch.

It was easy to tell the dog knew what was expected of him. He came right up and started to sniffing and getting excited. All I could remember was saying, "Oh God, No!"

I lunged with all the pent-up hatred and strength my body had ever known. Something had to give. My left hand came out of the shackles. The Mex guard with the submachine gun was standing just close enough, that when I lunged and swung my arm around in front of me, it brought that shackle around in an arc at lightening speed, and with the force of a sledgehammer. I didn't aim, I just swung. That chain and shackle wrapped around his head, and there was a sound like squashing a punkin with a rock.

Before he hit the ground, I grabbed that machine gun out of his hands and turned it on.

The first thing I did was cut that police dog to ribbons.

I'll say one thing for those drunk Mexicans. As drunk and passed out as they were, it didn't take long for them to get in action. There were several guns spitting flames at me by the time I'd finished with that dog.

But I didn't stop there. I didn't let up on the trigger of that gun. I just kept swinging it from one source of flames to another. Oh, how it did me good when, out of the melee, I recognized Rodriguez with a big sixgun booming in my direction. I could see my bullets cut through him and knock him backwards through the fire. I would have shot him more, but there were still other shots coming in my direction. I was getting so tired. I must have been hit several times already, but I wasn't aware of it. Kill every Mexican there, was all I could think. I kept that gun running full blast until it just completely ran out.

No shots were being fired at me. It was so quiet. Deathly quiet! I was so tired. The tiredest I'd ever felt in my life. And weak. God, how weak I was. Slowly I realized my shirt was wet and plastered to my body, what there was left of it.

The daylight had broken. It was not bright in the camp, but light enough to see around. I turned and stumbled to where Nan lay.

As I drug myself over to her, she raised a shackled hand weakly. I can remember reaching it with my left hand, and I noticed it was all skinned to pieces. Then she smiled faintly up at me and whispered, "My darling Booger Red."

I passed out with my cheek next to hers, and my body partly shielding her nude battered form.

Chapter X

THE LIVING DEAD

Unbeknownst to me, when I rode away from Senor Hernandez' ranch two years before, Lolita, my Mexican girl friend, had ridden out ahorseback following me to bring me back to the ranch. She rode the range a lot, and thought she knew all the wild, lonely places between their ranch and the border; but on that journey she followed me into country she'd never been in before.

When I was traveling across country, I always preferred the roughest, wildest, uncivilized country I could find, in preference to other places. That trip had been no different. I had really enjoyed it, on that trip north, as I had passed through country that I felt was the least populated, most remote country I had ever seen.

After a couple days following me, Lolita lost my tracks. She finally decided to circle back, cutting for sign to try to pick them up again. When the sun set in the wrong direction that evening, she suddenly realized she was lost, in a land she didn't know at all.

Her first panicky impulse was to kick her horse into a gallop and try to find the trail, in order to get herself straightened out. It was lucky for her that her horse was old and tired, and wise enough to quit running of his own accord.

It was completely dark by then. Her horse had stopped where there was a small patch of grass. Lolita still had a little grub and part of a canteen of water with her, so she did the only thing she knew. She hobbled her horse, tied her lass rope to the hobbles and to a stout bush; then tried to make herself comfortable for the night.

The next morning, with the first light of day, she rode off to try to get her bearings before it became too late and too hot.

She rode all that day with little food and water, without recognizing any familiar landmarks. That night, she was so tired and weak from hunger and the long ride, that she passed out when she lay down.

In the morning, the sun was burning into her eyes, and the music of goats blatting in her ears awakened her. She sat up, startled and thrilled. Rubbing her eyes, she tried to look at everything at once. Her mind told her, that where there were goats, there surely was a herder, and she would be saved.

She was brought wide awake by the sound of a strong young masculine voice.

"Buenos dias, Senorita."

There sat a wild, ragged, handsome young man, slightly older than she was. He was astride a wild Indian pony, as shaggy as he was.

After attending to her needs for food and water, the boy told her he came from a family of mixed Indian and Mexican blood. They ran a small herd of goats in the wild country for a living.

That boy was the one Lolita married a few months later. A couple of the vaqueros Senor Hernandez had sent to help us trail our steers north, had been his brothers.

On their way back to the rancho, they had ridden back by their mountain home to see their relatives. They had much to tell about the gringo friend of Lolita's and Senor Hernandez. He had brought his beautiful red-headed wife down to the ranch and had bought all Senor Hernandez' cattle. He had paid for it with gold, much gold; that they had seen with their own eyes. It was great good fortune for all the ranch. That summer had been very dry so far. The family had been forced to graze their goat herds out farther than they usually did. Unknown to them, they were close to the place Rodriguez had chosen for his camp. They were awakened just at daylight by the thunderous reports of heavy guns.

At first, spooked by the sound of shooting, the family started the herders to gather the goats off the bedgrounds and head up country away from the noise.

The younger men argued they should sit tight with the goats. They felt they should get their rifles and slip down the valley to see what all the commotion was, and find out what happened. Finally they convinced the older folks that was what they should do.

The young men had never been in this valley before, but the old "jefe", after studying the country close, recognized where they were. He told them years ago, there had been a bandido camp down the valley and up in a side draw a ways. He thought it had all been burned out in a raid by the policia.

Needless to say, the group of herders slipped up on the camp like drifting shadows.

When they were close enough to see the camp, they were startled to see a burned out campfire, surrounded by dead bodies everywhere they looked.

They worked their way all around the camp to make sure they weren't entering into a trap. Then they came in close to try to figure out what had happened.

The first they knew of Nanette and me being there was when they saw her beautiful red hair spread out on the ground. It was a terrible sight.

She was dead from internal bleeding. They could read the gruesome details of what had happened when they saw her nude body, with her hands still shackled around a post over her head.

At first, they thought I was also dead. There was a set of shackles on my right arm, and a badly warped, out of shape, machine gun still in my right hand.

There were twelve dead Mexicans there on the ground. One had a broken neck and one had his head bashed in. And one very dead dog.

When the herders started to move me, they discovered I was alive, but just barely. One young man was sent racing back to their camp to get help and medicine for me.

The others wrapped Nan's body in a blanket and gently laid her in a cool shady place, until they could prepare a decent grave for her.

As to the dead bandidos, they were stripped of their valuables, then drug off to a large depression where they were dumped together and covered up.

Those Mexicans lived out in the mountains all year round; and they did almost all their own doctoring. When they realized I wasn't dead, they weren't panicked by the distance to a doctor. They were used to caring for their own, and they knew all the old home remedies and herbs, which was lucky for me.

I had been shot full of holes, but no vital organs had been hit. Mostly the loss of blood, and the shock of the whole night was what almost did me in.

It was two weeks or more before I was conscious enough to realize I was still alive. It had been a close shave.

None of my nurses spoke English, and my command of the Spanish language wasn't good enough to allow me to converse very well with them. For quite awhile, it was difficult trying to understand them.

The first thing I asked about was Nan.

"La Senora Nanette?"

"Muerto y enterrado," was their solemn answer.

I almost gave up then. Life without Nan was worthless.

A long time later, something else came to mind.

"Cuantos bandidos muertos?" was my next concern. I was very disappointed when their answer was only, "Doce." Twelve. Then four had got away that night.

When I asked the next question, I guess I was hoping with all my heart and soul for the right answer. My words must have come haltingly as I spoke, "Senor Rodriguez muerto? Savvy?"

They looked blankly at me and answered slowly, "No savvy Senor Rodriguez."

I felt defeated, almost totally empty. I had to make them understand. I must be sure about Rodriguez.

I spent many days sitting there by that headstone, during the next few months.

I tried to describe him, but didn't know enough words. Then I recalled he was the only bandit with a heavy mustache. Finally they understood me.

"Ningun bandido muerto con mustachio!"

I think that is the only thing that kept me alive those first weeks. The thought that Rodriguez must have gotten away, and might still be alive. I made a solemn vow to myself right then, that I would never give up under any circumstances until I was positive beyond the shadow of a doubt that Rodriguez was dead. If I ever caught up with him in this life, I would kill him, even if I had to chew his jugular vein open with my own teeth to be sure.

It took a long time for me to heal up. Another month went by before I could even sit up in bed for any length of time. Part of the trouble was the terrible nightmares I had continuously of the events of that night. I would thrash around and kick so much, that I would tear one or another of the wounds open each time. There were times when I thought I'd go crazy with the pain of losing Nan. I would almost lose control of myself and give up; then I would remember Rodriguez, and my determination to live would flare up again.

Two months after the battle, I asked the boys to help me down to Nan's grave. It was quite an ordeal. When we got there, they showed me the simple grave, with a large granite headstone they'd chiseled out from the side of a mountain and hauled down to place on it. Carefully carved out in the center of the rock was one word, "Nanette."

I sank to the ground. They went away and left me alone. What I would have given to have been free to have joined her right then and there.

I spent many days sitting there by that headstone, during the next few months. Living in the past. Slowly mending both body and soul.

Then one day some vaqueros rode into camp. One of them was Lolita's brother-in-law. Word was passed to me that a wounded man answering Rodriguez' description had been seen riding north several months ago. More recently the same man had been seen across the border in West Texas.

I had sat and mourned long enough. My body was well. It was just the mind that had lingered. Now it was time for me to get on the trail. "Rodriguez' trail."

When I was preparing to leave, I asked my friends if they had an extra gun they might let me have, as I did not wish to go unarmed. They grinned and explained they had picked up all the guns from the dead bandidos at the battle. When they showed me their cache, I found my own .45 in their midst, the one Nan had given me for Christmas. I rode out with it strapped to my side.

When I got back in the States, the first thing I did was run into trouble. A big policeman stopped me and says, "Let me see your draft card, cowboy."

"What are you talking about?" was my startled answer. I'd never heard of a draft card and didn't know what one was.

The cop hustled me off to police headquarters where I had a heck of a time convincing the chief I didn't know a damn thing about what they were talking about. I was finally able to make them believe me when I showed them the freshly healed scars on my body, and told them I'd been hurt in an explosion in the remote mountains of Mexico, and had been sick nigh unto death for many months.

They finally explained to me that our country was at war. Much had happened those long months I was up in the mountains. I finally said, "Well, why in Hell didn't you tell me that when you first brought me in? I could have already been enlisted in the army if you'd have told me sooner."

Chapter XI

THE LONG WAR

Rodriguez was an American citizen. I figured I was just as apt to find him in the army as any other place. I joined the army the next day, thinking I'd probably get a chance to do a little "Rod" hunting before I saw any active duty.

A few weeks later I was on a boat heading for Europe.

They didn't ask me what I could do. They just stuck me in an ambulance and pointed out the driving course to me. I must have been in a hurry, thinking maybe I could get somewhere and find a list of names of all the men on the base. It seems I roared across the finish line, was jerked out of the ambulance, and ushered into a room full of other GI's and instructors, studying an advanced first aid course.

What free time I had there, I spent dead to the world; too tired to hold my head up. I was still weak from the shootout.

While there at that camp, I thought several times I should write to Sandy and Monte; but somehow I never found the time. It was roll out early every morning, take exercises, gulp down some grub; then run from one classroom to another all day. Study first aid, then mechanics, then running the advanced obstacle course under fire. Before I knew it, I had graduated and was on my way east.

I knew I should write Tom and Diana also; but each time I tried, I couldn't get past the opening sentence. I just couldn't bring myself to tell them Nan was dead, and how it happened. And that I hadn't caught up with the "cabron" that had done it. The longer I put it off, the harder it became.

I finally wrote Sandy and Monte. I told them simply that we had run into bad trouble in Mexico. Nan had died, and I had been hurt real bad. When I finally got back on my feet and returned to the States, the war was on. I had immediately joined the army and was shipping out. I promised to write more next time, after asking them to take care of Annabelle. I said I had named her on my insurance. I finished with the words, "I'll see you as soon as we wipe up this little squabble."

I also wrote to Larry and Mary O'Sulluvan, down in New Mexico. I told them quite a bit, and that I was on Rodriguez' trail. I asked them to check up on his relatives there to see if they could get a bead on him.

For some reason, I had forgotten to put my return address on the outside of the letter, which I remembered a few days after I'd mailed it. After thinking the matter over, I decided that it was probably lucky for me. Rodriguez had finally learned my name, and he was sure to have informed the folks in New Mexico what it was.

A couple months later when a letter, the first one I had received in the service, caught up with me; it was postmarked from Plush, Oregon. I knew something was up. The letter was from the O'Sullivans and was more of a book than a letter. They were tickled to death to hear from me, but so sorry to learn of all the tragedy.

After receiving my letter, they had checked around town amongst their Mexican friends. Rodriguez had indeed been back and had informed the officials of my true name. They had issued a warrant for my arrest for murder. It was Rodriguez' cousin I had fought that night in the barroom brawl, and he had died. Rodriguez also told them I had recently ambushed and murdered ten or eleven of his comrades, while traveling down in old Mexico.

Mary said the officials had tracked me to Tom's ranch in Arizona, but had been unable to find out anything further as to my whereabouts.

Mary then sent the letter for me enclosed in a letter to some of her relatives near Plush, and asked them to send it on to me. She was afraid if she mailed it to me from down there, some postal clerk might see it and recognize the name.

Mary also mentioned that Rodriguez was in the service and had shipped overseas as far as she could find out. It would indeed be a pleasure I'd enjoy, should I catch up with him somewhere in Europe.

After rereading the letter several times, I knew I'd have to write Tom and Diana, and also to Sandy and Monte again. There were several things I needed to say to them.

Writing that letter to Tom and Diana nearly tore me to pieces, but I finally got through it and got it in the mail. I told them the story, but left out the vulgar part. I just stated that we'd been captured by Rodriguez and his bandidos and held for ransom. I had broken loose and we'd had a shootout. I mentioned that several of the outlaws had been killed, but Rodriguez had gotten away. It was terribly hard to tell them that Nan had died in the battle; and that I was wounded and unable to care for her, but I did say we had been together when she died.

I tried to explain that it had taken several months for me to pull myself back together. As soon as I returned, I had joined the service, to try to follow Rodriguez' trail.

I tried to explain about the trouble between Rod and me. How his cousin had been killed that night in the bar, and now Rod had been able to get warrants out for my arrest.

I explained about leaving Annabelle with friends up north. Apparently Rod didn't know about her. I felt it was best for her safety to be left hidden out of reach, until I got ahold of Rodriguez and got my accounts settled up with him. I mentioned I had made a vow to get Rodriguez for what he had done. I sent no return address, and asked them not to try to locate me or Annabelle, for her safety. I promised to return when the war was over, and I caught up with Rod.

The letter to Sandy and Monte was much the same. In it, I told them some about Rodriguez, and asked them to raise Annabelle as their own daughter and to give her their last name for her own safety. I said if they got a chance to sell the ranch at a good profit, and wished to do so, it would help to hide the trail by moving to another state. I sent my return address on the inside of the letter, as I had done with the O'Sullivans, and asked them to be careful about sending me a letter.

I was sure Rodriguez would be as interested in locating and silencing me, as I was in finding and exterminating him.

The war got rough, and we were on the move constantly. Being an ambulance driver, I was always on the go. It was several months before another letter caught up with me. This was from Monte."

"Annabelle, I almost broke down and cried when I opened up that letter, and found a picture of you inside. Even as a little girl, you looked so much like your mother. I could hardly stand it. It brought that night back so clear again."

"There was lots of news in the letter.

They had tried to locate me after my first letter, but hadn't had any luck.

When Nan and I didn't catch up with them by the time they'd got the cattle up to Montana, they decided that we must have taken the pack trip into the hills.

A month later they were real worried, but figured we'd surely show up any time. Two months later Sandy couldn't stand waiting any longer so he headed south to look for us. On the way he stopped over night in Albuquerque. To pass the time that evening, he picked up a newspaper and was reading it. He came across a story about a cowboy that had jumped a group of Mexicans down in old Mexico, and shot up the bunch pretty bad. The Mexican authorities were looking for him, but hadn't located him yet. Sandy went on down to old Mexico and hunted for me until he ran out of money. He finally decided I was holed up somewhere and that I'd probably show up in Montana as soon as the racket blowed over. He told Monte that if I didn't show up later on, he'd go back and look some more. Then he was drafted into the army before he ever got to go south again.

Sandy was in Europe too.

What I would give to set and share a smoke with him again, I thought.

"My God, Sandy, I've found you at last!"

Monte had hung onto the ranch for awhile, but had found it very difficult to run with no help, an ailing mother, and two small children. When another outfit offered to buy her out; lock, stock, and barrel, she took them up on it and moved to Portland. She had sold everything except old Buck. She hauled him with her, and had him boarded out.

Since I'd been in the army, I'd learned a lot about finding out the names of all the men in all the camps where I was. Whenever I came across a name of Rodriguez, I'd really get chargy, and check it out every way I could. Several of them could have been the one I was looking for, but always when I came face to face with them, it would be the wrong Rodriguez.

I hunted for Sandy from then on too, but didn't have any luck there either for a long time.

The fighting didn't end right away like some of the fellows figured it would. One winter ran on into another, and another. It seemed like forever. It got to the point where I couldn't remember when we hadn't been fighting; and all my days were filled with wounded bodies, and shells flying overhead and exploding.

I checked out names and faces in England, Africa, Italy; and then finally I was sent to France. I'd never found the right Rodriguez; never met up with Sandy.

Then early in the last winter...

We'd been on the offensive, and chasing the Nazis like mad. Our boys had advanced faster than supplies and reinforcements could keep up.

I'd just recently joined the outfit as it was on the advance. I hadn't had a chance to do much name or face checking. Driving that ambulance kept me on the go. I just went where I was sent, picked up a load of wounded men, brought them back to a field hospital; then lit out again for the front lines to be ready for the next slaughter.

Things looked bad to me. It looked like the men I was tailing were getting into enemy territory without a rear cover. About that time, the retreating army turned and swooped down on us, bottled us up, and cut us off from our reinforcements. The fighting was ferocious. They were shelling the devil out of us and pouring .50 caliber machine gunfire in on us from every direction.

I couldn't get out with my ambulance; so the best I could do was try to make it from one wounded man to another, to administer whatever first-aid I could.

Long before the siege was over, my ambulance took a direct hit from a big shell, and was blowed off the face of the earth. There was no way out for me. I never could figure out how I kept from being hit, as I made it from hole to hole, doing what little I could.

I had seen a fellow off to my left get hit, and heard him yell for a medic. Just as a shell hit close by, which puffed up a good dust cover, I made a dash over to the wounded man. I slid into the hole beside him, and looked square into the eyes of Sandy!

"My God, Sandy, I've found you at last!"

He was wounded bad, but he was conscious, and he recognized me. He reached up and took hold of my hand.

"Howdy Pard. Got a smoke on you?"

"You bet." I fumbled out part of a sack of Bull Durham, and with shaking fingers rolled two smokes. I got his going and stuck it between his lips.

I was all thumbs as I tried to patch up his wounds and stop the bleeding.

Pretty soon he put his hand on my arm and says, "Sit down Pard, and talk to me before it's too late. Tell me what happened to Nan and don't leave nothing out."

It was hard to do, to bring all the gruesome details back to mind, and tell them to Sandy, but that's what I did. Everything I could remember, just the way it happened; and there at the last how I vowed to settle the score with Rodriguez if it took all my life.

Sandy had his hand on my arm when I finished. He pulled me down closer where he could look straight into my eyes.

"Pard, promise me you'll track that rat down and get him, even if you have to trail him to the far corners of the earth."

"You have my solemn promise, Sandy. That has been the only

thing that has kept me going; my only purpose in life."

Sandy had a good head on him. Even though he was badly wounded, his mind was clear; and he knew what he was saying and doing. He reached up and took off his dog tag and held it out to me; then went on.

"Red, I know I'm about done for. You take this dog tag and give me yours. That way you'll have an edge on the cur. If he ever checks the record, he'll find you got killed in action; but using my name, you can get him."

At that time, it seemed like a good idea. I was thinking only of hunting down Rodriguez. It didn't occur to me at the time, of the complications it would cause, taking Sandy's name, with him being married to Monte.

Sandy wouldn't settle down until I'd agreed to his plan, and we'd traded ID's. Every time he'd move, the blood would gush out worse. We had just gotten squared away, when another shell hit very close, and I was slammed into near eternity!

Chapter XII

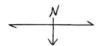

THE HOMECOMING

What happened next I'm not sure, but a couple weeks later, I woke up in a base hospital over on the coast. I guess I had a bad case of shell shock. It was a long time after that, before I really snapped out of the stupor I was in, and started to thinking for myself again. By that time, the damage had been done.

On my bed chart, I was listed as "Sandy". Then I remembered. I looked down at my dog tag. It also read "Sandy".

There were several letters there on my wash stand from Monte. I finally picked up the most recently postmarked one, opened it, and started reading.

Monte had received word from the War Department, that I, Daniel MacIntosh, had been killed in action. That's when the complications started.

It was such a problem on my mind, the army doctors must have thought I'd cracked up. I guess I'd read your letters over, Monte; then go into a trance, trying to figure out what to do. How could I break the sad news to you, that it was Sandy who'd gotten killed, not me.

I didn't talk it over with anyone, just kept mulling it over myself. Finally one day a nurse came in and told me to get packed up; they were shipping me back to a place in Virginia where there was a big hospital and better doctors. She assured me they'd get me well in no time.

While coming home on the boat, I finally got up enough nerve to write Monte. I left out the gruesome details of his condition, but I did tell her about finding Sandy, and telling him the story of Nan. He had insisted on our switching ID's. I had done it to pacify him, thinking I'd switch back as soon as I got him some help, but a shell had exploded and blown all my plans away; so now I had his name. It wasn't a very good letter, and I didn't know if she could understand it or not, but it was the best that I could do.

I didn't tell Monte I was coming back to the States; so I was home and out of the hospital before she knew about it. The army gave me a furlough first; then came through with a discharge quite awhile later.

When I got out, I was lost. I didn't know what to do. I guess I must have walked every street in town before I wound up at the train depot one day. The next thing I knew, I had a ticket for Portland, Oregon, and was on my way.

I wanted to see you, Annabelle, and I guess I wanted to talk to someone I knew. Monte was the only person I could remember knowing right at the time.

It was a beautiful spring day when I got off the train in Portland. I finally got up enough nerve to call the phone number Monte had written in the last letter she'd sent to Sandy. She'd told him about the apartment she was living in, and how it even had a telephone; so some night when he was setting out in his old foxhole, to give her a jingle. She'd be right close by to answer it.

When I dialed the number and the phone rang, I was very surprised when Grandma Cook answered. I didn't tell her who I was, but did manage to find out where Monte was working, which was in a large office building downtown, not very far from the train depot.

I guess I walked by that building a dozen times, before I finally got up enough nerve to go inside. As I entered the lobby, the first thing I saw was a clock that said it was straight up noon. Off to the left was a sign over a doorway which read "Cafeteria". When I turned and looked to the right, there stood Monte, standing frozen in her tracks!

I just stood there, looking at her; scared half to death, for I don't know how long. Finally I reached out toward her and blundered out, "Could I buy you a cup of coffee, Monte?"

Suddenly, she was in my arms, crying and hugging me, and getting my uniform all wrinkled and tearstained. Ours wasn't a reunion of lovers, but of old cherished friends meeting again.

We were creating a spectacle. Several other secretaries and workers in the building were on their way to lunch, and had to pass us to get to the cafeteria.

I held Monte away from me and asked her if we could get out of there for awhile. I'd noticed a quiet little park up the street a ways; so asked Monte if we couldn't go up there and sit for awhile. She looked around and saw a girl she knew, and asked her to tell her boss she couldn't work the rest of the day.

The gal replied, "Sure, Monte, go ahead. I'll tell the Old Man. You lucky gal! We'll cover for you."

We sat in the park a long time talking before we realized we'd missed lunch. Monte said it was too late to eat in a restaurant; so come on home with her and she'd cook supper for me. I needed her company right then as much as she needed mine. I also wanted to see my little Annabelle.

You were scared to death of that strange man in the uniform, Annabelle, but you soon got over it. It didn't take long to get you to ride my foot like a pony, when I crossed my legs and bounced you.

Little Danny took right to me. He just knew I was his daddy, come home.

I slept on the sofa that night, and for the entire month of my furlough.

Grandma Cook was thrilled to see me; but just couldn't figure it out, how they'd gotten Sandy and me mixed up in the service.

When I checked in with the army again, surprisingly enough, they made arrangements for me to see a doctor right there nearby in Vancouver. I was one of the first soldiers that had been in the war, to get a discharge. That is, Sandy was.

Spring had worn into summer by that time. I'd regained all my equilibrium, and my long interrupted purpose returned as well. I was getting restless. It was time to get on Rodriguez' trail. I hadn't told Monte much, but she knew what was in my mind.

I didn't know what to do about Monte. Legally, we were man and wife, and were living in the same house; but we weren't sharing the same bedroom.

I could hardly stand the thought of leaving her though.

One cool beautiful moonlight night in June, Monte and I went for a walk to a nearby park, where there was a good view of Mt. Hood. It was beautiful to sit and watch the moonlight reflected on that magnificent snow-capped mountain.

I'm not sure, but I think she brought up the subject that night; that we should do something, like moving back to a ranch.

"After all," she said, "I still have the money from the sale of the ranch and cattle in Montana, and over half of it belongs to you."

It seemed like a good idea to me; so I turned to her and took her in my arms and made a little speech.

"Monte, there is no other person alive that could take your place with me. We've both had a bad jolt in our lives, and I still have a terrible score to settle. But Dammit, Monte, what I'm trying to say is, we're supposed to be man and wife; so will you marry me and make it legal? We'll slip off down to Nevada and get married under my right name; then go out in eastern Oregon or Nevada somewhere and buy us a ranch and live as Sandy and Monte."

She stood and heard me through, looking at me from arm's length. Then a tear came into her eye. Slipping her arms up around my neck, she pulled me down to her. That was the first time I had kissed her since the day we'd met in the office building downtown.

It was settled. Monte quit her job, and we slipped off to Nevada and got married legally. From then on we lived together as Monte and Sandy. It was hard for me to get used to being called Sandy, and even tougher on Monte to have to call me that.

After our marriage, we went ranch hunting, in Nevada, Idaho, and Oregon. We finally located this place here on the Snake River

216

breaks, where we've lived ever since. It is hidden and remote, and that is what I was looking for.

I've been so busy telling about Monte and myself, that I left out something—old Buck. Monte had brought him to Portland with her and had him stabled out. When I asked her about him, she couldn't keep from grinning.

"You know what a one man/one woman horse he always was. Well, when I brought him here, he became even worse. If I'm not out at the stable to care for him, the man there just dumps his feed and water in his lot and leaves him alone. Buck won't have anything to do with him, and he won't let anyone in his lot with him. The guy out there just can't believe it when I come out and Buck follows me around without even a rope on him. I wonder if he'll still know you?" she asked.

The day Monte took me to see him was interesting. Monte called him and walked over to his pen where he was waiting to greet her. I walked to the pen several feet away and stood and called, "Buck, come here."

He raised his head and turned it partly toward me. He cocked his ears in my direction, so I called again.

"Come on, Buck, you old son of a gun."

He was very interested as he stood shaking his head up and down. I kept talking to him as I climbed over the fence and into his lot. He stood there watching me for a long time; then came walking slowly over to me and sniffed my outstretched hand. After a few seconds, he stepped closer and raised his nose up to my chin. He nuzzled me gently on the chin, then dropped his head slightly and just stood there looking at me as I talked to him and gently rubbed his ears.

I had to stand there quite awhile to regain my self composure. Old Buck did remember me, and he was glad to see me back. We've spent many happy days together since then.

When we bought the ranch, we made a deal to take immediate possession. As soon as we could drive to Portland, we loaded up you kids, Grandma Cook, Monte's things and old Buck, and we moved out here.

I guess I must have sort of half forgotten Rodriguez there for awhile. I never really completely forgot him. It was the strain of war; losing Sandy, coming back to Monte, with all the changes that followed, that caused me to put him in the back of my mind for that summer.

All good things seem to end. In the middle of the night one time, Monte woke me up finally by throwing cold water on me. She said I was thrashing and ranting and raving so much that she was getting real worried. It took me awhile to settle down. I finally told Monte it was the war I was reliving. I didn't have the nerve to tell her what I hadn't told her before. It was that night down in old Mexico that was tearing me up.

I never slept any of the rest of that night; just sat and drank coffee and tried to figure out what I should do. By morning, I knew I had to go to New Mexico to see Larry and Mary. I had to get back on Rodriguez' trail or I'd never rest again.

It was heartbreaking to leave Monte and you kids the next day. I have felt guilty time and again for doing it, and have been thankful to Monte a million times for not holding it against me, or getting angry at me when I went off and left her alone that way. But every so often, I had to do it to hold myself together.

I think Monte knew I wasn't telling her the truth. When she came in, I was packing a small satchel. I didn't know she was watching me until I turned to leave. There was an awful lonesome look in her eyes as she spoke. She betrayed her thoughts with a slip of the tongue when she said, "Red, if you have to use that .45, be careful, and come back."

That first trip I went straight to New Mexico to see Larry and Mary. I hadn't written to them in almost a year and hadn't heard from them in almost that long. I found out later that their last letters to me had been returned unclaimed. I had been killed in the war...

I arrived in New Mexico disguised as a traveling salesman. It had occurred to me I had better not show my face around town.

Mary was working in the yard, and Larry was sitting on the porch, that day, when I walked up to their place.

"Joy and begorry, those be the prettiest flowers I've seen this side of Dublin, me lovely lassie," in my best Scotch-Irish brogue.

Mary looked up and came right back at me.

"Aye, and it's a sure bet I'll make, ye've niver even crossed the River Mississippi."

"No Ma'am," I said in my natural tongue, "but I've been in Warner Valley a time or two."

"Can we go inside?" I asked, as I held out my sample case, "I'll show you my wares," I whispered, "and I'll tell you some news that's hard to believe."

We sat and talked way late that night. They wanted to know everything that had happened to me since that night I'd ridden out with Blizzard and Buck. I told them the whole story before I asked them if they had any news about Rodriguez.

Mary brought me a fairly new newspaper. It had a story in it about Rodriguez coming home, a decorated "hero". It went on to say that he would be traveling down near Houston, Texas, to take a position with some large company as a security officer in charge of a large group of men.

I knew I'd soon be heading for Houston, but right then I decided to stay right where I was for the time being. At least until I got that breakfast I'd promised to have with them so many years ago.

I wrote Monte and told her not to worry about me, and to try not to be angry with me for being gone. Some day when it was over, I'd tell her all about it.

I spent a week in Houston before I got a lead. A fellow answering his description had boarded an airplane headed for Chicago, while I was at the airport.

A long week in Chicago left me tired and disgusted, with no results. I finally decided I'd better give up the hunt for awhile, and go help Monte take care of the ranch. I got a ticket for the next flight out.

The passengers were all on our plane, and I guess they were closing the hatches, as the passengers from an incoming plane walked by.

I was sitting next to the window, looking out at nothing in particular, mostly just thinking how I'd neglected Monte and the ranch. Suddenly I noticed one of the men in the group had stopped and was looking directly toward me. He was a handsome, clean shaven city-dressed feller. It took awhile for me, but gradually in my mind, I put a shaggy mustache and rough cowboy clothes on him. As the motors of the plane revved up and it shot forward, recognition shot through to both of us. That was Rodriguez, and he knew me!

I was on my feet, shouting to stop the plane; I had to get off. The man on the ground went running toward some other guys that looked like airport officials, waving his arms and yelling too. Then we were gone down the runway.

The plane was roaring so loud no one paid any attention. About that time, we became airborne. Some big guy across the aisle got through to me by then.

"Shut up, cowboy. We're on our way, and this baby won't light 'till we get to Omaha."

Sometimes it is hard to accept things the way they are, but there wasn't much I could do but just set and wait.

Before we got to Omaha, I had worked things around, trying to figure out what Rodriguez was thinking and doing when he ran to the officials on the ground. It finally occurred to me, he meant to have me arrested to answer his old New Mexico murder warrant. Damn!

I couldn't let him find me. The law being what it was, they might grab me and do me in before I ever got the slightest chance at that Rodriguez.

Now, the hunter was being hunted!

I had to think up a whole new line of strategy. First, shake Rodriguez, and then get back on his trail again.

Lucky for me, I'd signed on the plane under an alias which I'd gotten identification for down in Texas. Even luckier, I'd brought city clothes along in my hand bag which I'd packed on the plane with me.

The plane I was on flew to Salt Lake City, with stops in Omaha and Cheyenne on the way. Since I would have to change plane companies in Salt Lake, that was as far as I bought the ticket. I'd thought about riding the bus from there on the rest of the way.

I decided if Rodriguez really had recognized me, and had been able to convince the police of anything, that they would probably be waiting to board the plane in Omaha to check it out. The best thing I could do would be to get into those city clothes and try to slip by them in Omaha.

There was a restroom at the rear of the plane, where I made my switch. I sure hated to roll my good cowboy hat up and cram it into that little satchel, but I didn't want to leave it there, and it was a dead giveaway on my head.

The plane wasn't fully loaded; so after I made the change, I came out and sat in a rear inside seat.

There were a few passengers to unload in Omaha. When we landed, I saw a police car sitting up by the passenger loading zone. There were two cops standing out by the loading area, as the plane door was opened, and the ramp rolled in place.

I was the first person out of the plane and down the ramp. I smiled at the cops as I passed by.

I chanced a glance back as I entered the building amidst a waiting crowd. I was just in time to see the last passengers come down the ramp and the cops go up it. I didn't panic and run, but I sure didn't stick around to find out if they found what they were looking for.

I slipped out of the airport area, crossed the road, and made my way down into the brush that ran around the north side of the little lake there. I found a secluded spot and spent the afternoon.

Rodriguez was now on my trail. Even though the name on the plane register didn't jibe, Rodriguez knew as well as I did, that we had seen each other. Neither of us would be satisfied until the other was done for.

It looked like the best thing for me to do was to go back to the ranch and disappear for awhile. Maybe after he got tired of hunting me, I might be able to get him.

He had the law on his side, even if it was all crooked and one-sided. I was dead as far as the world was concerned; so if Rodriguez couldn't find me and prove any different, he had a poor chance at me.

Late that night, I walked around the end of the lake and down toward the train yards. I caught a west bound freight train, heading out.

That evening before boarding the train, I'd stopped in a little "Greasy spoon" restaurant and wolfed down a good meal, which I was beginning to need. While eating, I picked up a newspaper lying on the counter, and was idly browsing through it. I came to a story about the local police being summoned to the airport that morning to intercept an airplane on a flight from Chicago to Salt Lake City. They were looking for a possible murder suspect that was believed to be on the plane. A security officer had seen the man on the airplane in Chicago just prior to takeoff; but before he could alert authorities the plane was airborne.

The description given could have fit any number of six foot, red-headed cowboys. I was glad I still had my city dude disguise on though.

I stayed out of sight and didn't have any trouble making it out to western Nebraska the next morning, where I saw a good chance to jump off the train unnoticed as it slowed for a town.

I found a stream and cleaned up before walking into town to find something to eat. It seemed to me that town had lots of cops and they all gave me the once over. It was hard to keep from leaving before I got a meal, but I stuck it out, and then picked up a sack of groceries to carry me over three or four days.

I stayed out of sight again as much as possible until after dark. Then I walked back to the railroad and caught another freight west again.

A big full, yellow moon was flooding down on the prettiest, homiest-looking ranch headquarters I could ever imagine.

I had lots of time to think for the next couple of days. It was hard not to double right back and get on Rodriguez' trail and try to nail him."

"Annabelle, if it hadn't been for you kids and Monte, I'm sure I would have done just that. That summer I'd gotten very attached to little Danny also. That little guy of Monte's and Sandy's was quite a boy, and he was sure I was his daddy."

"I just couldn't take a chance of Rodriguez getting me cornered by the law and putting me out of commission while he went free. My desire and determination to get him was no less. If possible, it hurt me even more to think of him being in a position of security guard authority, and me unable to do anything, but I had to think of my family. I would just have to figure out some new strategy.

There was a chance he might be able to figure out what was supposed to have happened to me in the service. He might even stumble on to the possibility that I had changed ID's with a dead soldier, but I could think of no way he could find out what the man's name might be. On the other hand, who knows?

It still seemed best to me to get back out to our remote ranch, let the trail blow over, and then start out again.

The train tracks were about twenty five miles across country from the ranch, and on a grade. Where they start up over the high country, the old freights would pull way down slow, climbing to the top. When my "side door Pullman" chugged her way up that grade, I bailed off and rolled down through the sagebrush. I waited and watched as it slowly chugged on out of sight.

That twenty-five miles across country is a long hike when you're coming home. It seemed I walked and walked and still never got anywhere. Part of the trouble was that I got to worrying about Monte and you kids. What if something had happened to you while I was gone? I could never forgive myself for going away and leaving you. Or what if Monte had become angry or disgusted with me for being gone so long and not keeping in touch with her? If Monte was fed up with me and refused to have anything to do with me, I just wouldn't know what to do. At times like that I would almost break into a run to try to cover the miles quicker.

Night time arrived before I got home. As I topped the last ridge, I was greeted by a beautiful sight. A big full yellow moon was flooding down on the prettiest, homiest looking ranch headquarters I could ever imagine.

There was a light on in the house. As I approached, I caught a movement out by the corral fence behind the house. There was someone sitting on the fence, watching my approach. My heart skipped a beat. I was sure it was Monte, and she wasn't coming to meet me.

I stopped, with my body tingling, and all my nerves on fire. She wasn't coming to meet me. What was wrong? Then I knew. Dumb me! I still had my city clothes on.

"Monte, is that you?"

She slid off the fence and stood leaning back against it, holding out her arms. In a weak, husky voice, she said, "Red, is that you? I almost took a shot at you. Where'd you get those city clothes?"

Then she was in my arms, holding on to me so tight. All my worries that she wouldn't want me back were gone, but I couldn't have blamed her if she hadn't.

We talked a long while. Then Monte turned me to where the moonlight showed full on my face. Looking up at me, she asked,

"Did you get him, Red? Is it all over?"

"What are you talking about Monte? What makes you say something like that?"

"I know what took you away."

"How?"

"Those terrible dreams you have. Sometimes you talk in your sleep."

She pulled herself closer to me and laid her head against my chest.

"I'm sorry, Monte," was all I could say. " I didn't want to worry you with my troubles. Let's just try to forget it for awhile."

Life was good then. We stayed there on the ranch and enjoyed it for a long time.

Chapter XIII

MEMORIES OUT OF THE PAST

I'd build to them, ride right into their midst, and rope a good stout young one, and the battle would be on.

I had to put Rodriguez out of my mind, to be able to stay there on the ranch, knowing he was still alive. Sometimes it would get to bothering me too much, and I would get moody. Then I'd go saddle one of our good Thoroughbred cross horses, slip out in the badlands, and scout around until I located a band of mustangs. I'd build to them, ride right into their midst, and rope a good stout young one, and the battle would be on. Usually it would be such a fight that it would take all my faculties and strength to get the bronc down and hogtied. I'd transfer my saddle to him, turn him loose, and slip into the saddle as he sprang to his feet.

By the time I'd get him to handling good enough to ride him back to the ranch, I'd be so worn out that the thought of Rodriguez still kicking around wasn't bothering me so bad. I could live with it again for awhile.

I used an old horse called "High Pockets" on most of those chases, and he sure was a good one. As long as I left a bridle on him with a long mecate, he'd stay right with me on those mustangs. That always helped to get the mustangs home.

The first one I caught like that was way down on the desert about thirty or forty miles below here. It was quite a battle, and we'd torn up quite a bunch of sagebrush before I finally got him headed back toward the ranch. We hadn't gone too far when we topped over a ridge. I spotted what looked like a sheriff's pickup, stopped down on the flats. There was a man a short ways from it, walking up the desert trail. I wasn't anxious to face up with any sheriffs, but from where we were, it was a long ways to any other ranch or town.

The man spotted me coming his general direction quite awhile before I was able to haze that mustang down to where he was. When I finally got within talking distance, he told me the motor in his pickup had blowed up. He'd run the battery down trying to get somebody on the radio, but he hadn't had any luck. He said he had his saddle with him, as he'd been out at a ranch; so I told him to see if he could get up to old High Pockets. If he could ride him, it would sure beat hoofing it.

That deputy sheriff was a pretty good cowboy. It wasn't everybody that came along, that could saddle High Pockets, much less ride him. I had already ridden that old devil forty or fifty miles that day, but when that feller, a total stranger, took ahold of him, you'd have thought he was a plumb fresh bronc.

It sure did me good to see that deputy twist him down, saddle him, and step on. Then he kicked off a few patches of hair as Mr. High Pockets came unwound. Of course, I didn't get to see all of it, as the commotion spooked my mustang and he blowed up again. I finally got him headed back toward the ranch, and after a bit, I see the deputy came galloping after me.

We didn't do much visiting on the way back to the ranch, and it was after dark when we rode in.

It sure looked good to see the light in the kitchen window, and to fill our nostrils with the smells of supper cooking on the old wood cookstove.

Monte heard us coming, and had the big corral gate open when we rode up. It took some persuading to get my mustang through it, but with the help of the deputy and High Pockets, we finally made it. What a relief it was to be somewhere that I could step off that bronc and not have to worry about him jerking away from me, or to have to battle him to get back on.

We'd gone in for supper before I thought to do any introducing.

You kids and Grandma Cook were all there. It was one of those funny times when you go to introduce someone and suddenly realize you don't know his name. All I could say was, "Deputy, I'd like you to meet my wife, Monte. Beside her is her mother, Mrs. Cook; my son, Danny, and my daughter , Annabelle. My name is Sandy."

The deputy said his name was Ray. You kids took right to him.

After supper, we drove him to town. That was the start of quite a friendship between us. I guess he's been out here to every branding and gathering and mustang chase since then that he could make. No one could take Sandy's place in our lives, but he made his own spot.

On the way to town that night, he told us he'd cowboyed and buckarooed throughout the West. He'd even put in a hitch for the "Portuguee" on the ZX before the war. He'd got a job as a deputy sheriff in our county after getting out of the army.

I didn't tell him much about myself. I didn't want him trying to connect me with anyone he'd known or heard of before the war.

Late one fall, after we'd shipped our steers, we decided to take a trip. Monte and I hadn't hardly been off the ranch for a long time. She hadn't really been away from it since we'd moved out there.

We didn't have any place in particular to go. We just wanted to get away for awhile, so we headed down to Reno. After a couple days there, we drove on down through Death Valley and on over to L.A. We decided we might like to spend a few days on the beach or maybe poke around Hollywood some.

The day we got to the film capital, one of the large movie production companies was holding an auction, selling off most of their western equipment.

It was quite a thrill to see all that equipment up close. Those wagons and buggies really interested us, and we decided we would stay and try to buy one.

As we worked our way past the big freight and covered wagons, my interest really perked up. There sat two stagecoaches, side by side in the line up.

The first coach appeared to be in much better shape than the second; so I spent quite awhile going over it, with the thought in my head how I'd sure like to drive one of them again. I'd fallen in love with that first coach before I ventured over to the other one.

When I walked near it, something came over me. It was almost like meeting an old friend I hadn't seen for years. I just stopped and stared at it from a short distance for a time before I could go on up to it. I could feel something as I walked all around it; past the rear boot and on up to the tongue, where I reached up and grabbed hold of the foot rest on the front boot. Stepping on the tongue, I pulled myself up to where I could look into the boot. There I froze! I was looking into the same front boot that I had looked into that day so many years before, when I had scrambled into it, gathering up the lines to try to get a runaway stagecoach under control!

There was a small "7" which had been burned into the wood on the front of the coach under the seat, which I'd noticed that day. I hadn't thought of it since. I don't know how long I stood there looking at that "7", thinking back. I must have been pale, for Monte finally reached up and shook my arm and asked me if I was alright.

"Yeah," I answered, trying to smile, "I just bumped my crazy bone."

I didn't say much about the coach, but I knew I'd buy it one way or the other.

We bought the buggy Monte liked, and then I told her I wanted to stay and see the coaches sell. I got the coach, and had to pay a stiff price for it, but sweet Monte never got onto me about it.

Now you know why at different times, I have acted so strange about that coach, when I was around it or talking about it. It and I were partners a long, long time ago.

We rented a big trailer and hauled our prizes back to the ranch. It took quite a lot of work and material to restore the old coach, but by the time I had six head of horses working together well enough to trust putting them on the coach, I had it ready to go.

Ray, our deputy friend, showed up that first day I hooked the six head to the coach. He was sure thrilled. I took advantage of his being there, and got him to ride out on a good saddle horse with us until the horses settled down, just in case they spooked and tried to run away.

It took several miles of traveling hard before those horses really settled down good on the coach. It sure was a thrill to be back up there on that driver's seat; to feel the swing and sway of the coach, and the tugs and pulls of the lines as the fresh air briskly whipped by. As we did all our ranch work with horses, I had quite a bunch to pick from. It wasn't long until I had a really good stagecoach hitch put together.

I didn't plan on taking the coach and hitch off the ranch, but Ray just couldn't be convinced that I didn't want to take it to town. He insisted I should bring it in for the local rodeo and parade. I tried to explain to him these were just desert horses, and hadn't any of them hardly seen a town or heard the city noises. The only answer I could get out of the man was, "There's a way to get them used to it."

I finally gave in.

We built a large arena and decorated it with all kinds of flags and obstacles we could come up with. Ray brought out his sheriff's pickup and drove it with the blinking red lights, siren blaring and horn blowing.

We finally decided it was safe to take the horses to town for some real city exposure. We still had a week before the parade, when we moved into the fairgrounds and started our finishing course on the hitch.

Ray produced a couple other mounted cowboys to ride out with us. We had our hands full several times those first few days, but we kept after them, driving them in all kinds of city predicaments. By the time the parade rolled around, we had an excellent handling, well-behaved stagecoach hitch to lead the parade. It was lots of fun, and there was a lot of publicity, which I really didn't want. I didn't want any pictures of me out in public.

I still had bad times when I'd get to brooding over Rodriguez. For several years, I'd slip off from time to time, to try to pick up his trail again. I followed false leads all over, just as in Europe during the war. There was a frustrating trip to South America, and a wild goose

233

chase through the Orient, but always the Rodriguez I was trailing had vanished or moved on before I got there. I just didn't seem to be able to get a lead on him anywhere anymore. I still kept in contact with the O'Sullivans down in New Mexico, but they hadn't heard any news of him either.

Poor Monte. How she hated to see me get into one of those black moods, knowing I'd finally take off again. But, bless her, she knew I had a job to do, and she never got after me for it. She never failed to welcome me back, no matter how hard it had been on her.

Cow ranching has never been a real good financial business, but finally along in the early fifties, prices started picking up. It looked to me like the way things were going, that we'd have good enough income that I might be able to take off a couple months or whatever time I needed, to get back on his trail and settle the score.

Then something went wrong in the cow market that fall. Steers that we had contracted to sell for forty-three cents finally brought sixteen to eighteen cents, and we were lucky to get that. There was no way I could go on the hunt that fall, if I was to try to hold our ranch together and take care of my family. As much as it hurt me, I had to give up the chase again.

A couple more years went by. One day Ray showed up, saying he had some good news for us. It seemed a big movie was going to be filmed not too far away, and a friend of his had called and asked him if he could locate some teams for it. Of course, Ray immediately thought of us. Taking it for granted we would be interested and could use the money, he made a deal for us.

After thinking it over, I decided it would be alright. I wouldn't be in the films, and probably wouldn't get any unwanted publicity out of it.

We went out on the movie set that summer, and had the first real treat away from the ranch in a long time. The livestock contractor for the movie had been an old time chuckwagon cowboy. We became well acquainted and good friends. We invited him and his family out to our ranch a couple weekends when they weren't filming.

During one episode of the movie, they had six head of horses on a freight wagon. The movie teamster just couldn't handle the horses and put the wagon and hitch where the director wanted it. Finally the director got mad and went to yelling about paying good money to get something and getting nothing for it. It got to the point where it riled my feathers, so I stopped the teamster and told him to get down off that driver's seat. I'd show that damn director how to drive that hitch and wagon right up his camera lens.

Those horses knew who had hold of them when I got up there. I gathered in the lines and squalled at them. I didn't even wait for the director to call "Action!" I just put them through their paces and right where he wanted them. As I galloped by on the last pass, I headed straight for the director at a dead run and swerved by him and his camera within inches, and yelled at him.

"There, damn you, could your old time drivers beat that, you old hot-headed buzzard?"

I never realized at the time, they had their cameras running full blast and trained right on me. It must have been what he wanted. When the movie came out, there I was galloping that hitch right across the screen, looking directly out at the crowd, and shouting something at somebody or other. They must have dubbed in another voice for mine, as it wasn't my voice or what I said. Anyway, there I was, big as Life!

It was a year after the filming before the movie came out, and that was a couple years ago.

In the meantime, we had kept up our friendship with the old cowboy who was the stock contractor. Last year, he and his wife stopped by and spent a few days with us again. Monte and I took them with us down on the desert and did a little filly chasing. We all had a good time.

I got a chance to haze a band of "shitters" over in his direction, and he was able to ride right into them. He roped a goodlooking bay yearling stud. With the four of us, there, it wasn't much of a job to get him forefooted, throwed, and tied up; and then put a hackamore on his head. Our contractor friend was as proud of that colt as an old hen with one chick, when he headed back to California with him.

Then just last week, out of a clear blue sky, I got two letters in the mail.

One of them was from that old cowboy. In it was a picture of that bay horse, a two year old now. He was standing there with a halter on, as fat and slick and contented looking as a good horse could be.

There was lots of news in the letter. At the end, he went on to mention that we might be getting a chance to sell some work horses pretty soon, if that dude that had come out to see him was really as interested as he seemed to be. This Mex had seen the horses in the movie, and he was putting a wild west show together down in Texas somewhere. He needed a hitch just like the one in the movie. Of course he'd gotten the livestock contractor's name off the movie screen. He'd come to California thinking maybe the horses were his and were located there.

That Mex had wanted to know if he had any pictures of the horses we had. When he was shown the pictures, one of them which showed more of a close-up of me than the horses, seemed to interest him greatly. The Mex had asked for the picture, but didn't get it.

The other letter was from a "Mr. Gentry," with an El Paso return address on it. It was from a man inquiring about work horses for sale. He was interested in something like the six-horse hitch he'd seen in the movie. He was willing to pay a premium price for quality. Also, there would be an opening for a good driver, in case I might be interested in the job, or perhaps might know of a qualified man for the position. He would like to have pictures of the horses for sale, and the driver, to be sure they fit together properly to fill his needs.

Mr. Gentry from El Paso! I'll bet he's not nearly as English as his name sounds.

I felt just like an old lobo testing the wind before starting out on an old trail.

Needless to say, I answered the letter, sending pictures of several teams and the hitches. I also sent along a couple pictures of myself, good shots, but where I had my face shaded just enough so that I was almost recognizable, but not for sure.

I also sent directions how to get out here to the ranch. I stated that I'd probably be working around close to the ranch for the next couple weeks, as I was starting some young horses, and should be easy to find.

Monte could tell that something was brewing, although I didn't tell her or let her see the letters.

For the past few days, I have whetted my senses and reflexes to a finer edge, just like a good knife. I have cleaned and checked my old .45 a dozen times or more; and that short double barreled shotgun has been kept loaded and within my reach at all times. I have climbed to that high place several times each day and night, studying the desert road that leads into here for any telltale sign of a dust cloud which means someone is approaching.

I packed a case of dynamite out by that big deep crevice in the lava rocks, and cached it, along with fuse and caps, so as to be ready for something. I could feel it in my bones.

I am sitting here with a high powered telescope in my lap, my .06 leaning on a rock on one side of me, and that scattergun on the other. My old .45, the one Nan gave me for Christmas so many years ago, is in my lap. I'm feeling at ease with the world, and prepared to do what must be done.

Raising the telescope to my eyes, I check out an approaching dust cloud. The maker of it seems to be driving slow, to keep the dust to a minimum.

The car isn't one I recognize, and the license plate seems to be a different color than ours is.

There is a last rise on the road just before dropping down into the ranch. I had marked it on the map I'd mailed out, so a stranger wouldn't think he was lost. Just before reaching this, the car stopped and one man got out. He carries a high powered rifle with a scope on it, and he turns and studies the country like a man intent on a sniping mission might do.

If that goodlooking man with the big, black mustache is an Englishman, then I've missed my guess.

That's enough writing for now.

Thanks to my telescope, I know what is approaching.

I sat on that rock and watched him walk right into my hands. I don't know why he didn't see me. I wasn't very well concealed.

When he was about twenty-five yards away, I stepped out in the opening, with nothing in my hands. Quietly, but demandingly, I called out to him.

"Rod!"

It crackled through the stillness with the same cold, icy hiss like I might have said, "rattlesnake!"

I went on.

"There was a time I would have killed you on sight, but now I want you to know what's coming to you. You low down, sneaking snake!"

I didn't know if he had his .06 loaded and ready, with the safety off or not, but I would have bet on it. All he had to do was swing it 90 degrees to have it pointed in my direction.

"Why don't you lay your air rifle down and get on your knees and say your prayers, you filthy "cabron", son of a whore?"

I stood there with a disgusted, snarling look, as he pretended to carefully start putting the rifle aside. Then quickly as a striking snake, he jerked the barrel toward me.

Before the arc was completed, my old pearl-handled .45 was out and bucking and bellering.

I didn't aim for a heart or head shot. I just wanted to wing him where it would hurt the most. My first shot slammed him right in the groin, down low. An instant later, my second shot busted the arm holding the rifle. It stifled a scream of pain as it spun him around and slammed him to the ground.

He came up with an automatic in his left hand. He nearly got me before I got a shot through that arm.

He was helpless then. I holstered my .45 and picked up the shotgun. Turning it toward him with both hammers pulled back, I said, "Get on your feet, sidewinder, before I blow out your guts right here!"

It was a good thing it wasn't very far up to that crevice in the rocks. I had my horse hid back up there in that cliff. Part of the way he staggered along, and part of the way I drug him.

He finally got up enough nerve to ask me where I was taking him.

"To your grave, scorpion. If you know any prayers, you better get on with them. You've been in this world way too long already. Now you are going to die, and I hope the thought of what you did to my wife chokes the very last breath out of you!"

It didn't bother me in the slightest to swing that double barreled 12 gauge toward his wishbone, and turn both hammers loose together. He'd never given Nan a chance at all, those many years ago, when he'd had her shackled to a post and had fifteen men to help him hold her. He'd had plenty of chance a little while before, when he'd come at me with a loaded automatic in his belt, and a cocked ready rifle in his hands.

Then he was dead, and I was just putting the finishing touches to the job. Even though I considered him vermin, I had to dispose of his carcass. Some people might not agree with me. That's when I wrapped the case of dynamite around his body, dropped it in the crevice, and set it off."

Chapter XIV

ALL ACCOUNTS SQUARED

When Monte finished reading, it got deathly quiet for a long while.

Annabelle was just sitting there, pale and sick looking. I didn't know what to think.

Finally she got up and came over to where I was sitting, worried to death over what she thought. She stood in front of my chair and looked directly at me, and whispered so low I could barely catch it.

"Daddy, may I sit in your lap before I fall?"

As I held my arms up to her, she dropped toward me, sobbing.

"Oh Daddy, please forgive me for doubting you today."

Then she was on my lap with her arms around my neck, crying like a small girl.

I looked up through tear dimmed eyes toward Monte. As I held out a hand, she also slid into part of my lap and was sobbing gently on my shoulder.

The story was repeated one more time for young Danny, when he came home from the service. After that, the subject of Rodriguez was never mentioned around our house again.

After a bit, I excused myself from my women, telling them I had some chores to take care of, and that I would be late getting home that night.

Rodriguez had left the keys in his car. As I cranked it up, I noticed an advertising type circular on the seat. It seems he was running for sheriff down in Texas.

I figured the reason he came after me alone, he was so sure of himself that he thought my capture dead or alive would really make him a hero in the eyes of his Mexican worshippers.

I took nothing out of the car. As a matter of fact, I had even walked back up on the ridge and picked up his rifle and automatic and put them in the car.

There was a spot I knew of where that car could be jumped over the cliff into the rapids of the Snake River way down below. It wasn't hard to get rid of, but it sure was a long walk back to the ranch.

About a year or so later, Ray made one of his usual stops by the ranch one day. He was now full sheriff of the county, as he'd taken over when the old sheriff retired.

He wanted to know if he and I could take a ride out on the desert a ways. He said he had something on his mind.

I asked if he had any particular place he wanted to go. His answer was, "No, just some place quiet where we can talk."

We rode up to a ridge I have always cherished, where you can gaze across the desert for miles and miles.

He got off his horse and made himself comfortable on a rock. Looking directly at me he says, "Sandy, I don't know where to start, but here are my conclusions of what might have happened.

You know, I think there might have been an old score settled here in these Snake River badlands, with the extermination of a real low down snake of an hombre."

I didn't interrupt him so he went on with his story.

"Several months ago, some fishermen discovered the remains of a car in the river down here quite a ways below the rapids. It was pretty beat up, but we had to investigate, and finally found a Texas license plate on it, which was registered to a deputy sheriff over in Texas.

When I wrote to the authorities down there, they answered, stating the owner of the car who was a candidate for sheriff at the time, had disappeared about a year ago. After checking with his friends, they believed he might have come up into this country hunting for a

244

murder suspect who had killed his cousin over in New Mexico many years ago.

The name of the little town rang a bell. Then I remembered it was the same town I'd seen on a letter I'd brought in to you from your highway mailbox. I even remembered the good Irish name on the return address.

I went back into our storeroom and started going through all the old wanted posters. I was about to give up about a month later, when I came across what I was looking for. It was a wanted poster from that same New Mexico town.

I finally got on a plane and flew down there. I went into town dressed as a cowboy, not a sheriff.

I visited with the O'Sullivans several days before Mary finally told me what had happened; first in the bar room brawl, then later down in old Mexico.

It seemed the man I was looking for, Danny something or other, had been killed in the war. This Texas deputy, not knowing his suspect had a friend who resembled him very much, had come up here looking for trouble. Apparently, some way or another, he met his just dues.

I guess until his corpse is found, no one could be charged with anything anyhow. Oh, Yeah, besides that, the rifle and a small handgun we found in his car still had exploded shells in the firing chambers.

You've told me quite a few wild stories through the years, and I just thought you might be interested in hearing this one. I'd say the buzzard that caused all the trouble for that feller, Danny, sure got what was coming to him. As far as my office is concerned, the case is closed."

I finally looked up at Ray and grinned.

"That sure was a wild sounding yarn, Ray. Maybe you ought to get some writer to make a novel out of it sometime!"

THE END

As far as my office is concerned, the case is closed.

GLOSSARY

Cowboy Terms

Busting
: Knocking the legs out from under an animal and flipping it in the air hard enough when it falls to knock the wind out of it.

Cabron
: (Spanish): Goat; An obscenity when applied to humans; the lowest form of life.

Chinook
: Soft warm spring breeze

Chivaree
: (French) var.: charivari, shivaree: a mock ceremony for newlyweds; Various forms of fun designed to prevent newlyweds from being alone

Classing up
: Sorting according to type

Dallied
: (Spanish - dar la vuelta): to turn around; to wrap the rope around the saddle horn when roping

"dobe"
: Adobe: mixture of mud and straw used in the Southwest to make building bricks or blocks

Forefooted
: Catching a horse by the front feet with a figure eight loop, which generally tumbles them to the ground

Ganted up
: Gaunt; flattened stomach or flanks due to lack of water or food

Houlihan	Var. hoolihan; a special type of backhand throw which cowboys use, especially for catching horses, usually having a small loop.
Jerky	Deer meat (venison) cut in thin strips and dried over a fire
Jigger boss	Second in command under the wagon boss if there is one, or, if not, under the cow boss
Jimmycane	Whirliwind; swirling, funnel-like, desert dust cloud
Jingled	Var.; Jangled; bringing in the horses
Lass rope	Lasso; a cowboy's rope
Line camp	Simple camp on the outside boundary line of a ranch where cowboys stay to keep their cattle inside the line and the neighbor's cattle out
Maverick	Unbranded or unmarked cattle
Mecate	(Spanish) Var.; McCarty; hair rope that is used as the reins and lead shank in connection with a hackamore
On the hook	Angry; fighting mad
Piggin' string	Short rope or leather strap used to tie an animal's feet together to prevent it from standing up
Powwow	Conference; group discussion
Remuda	(Spanish), exchange; Group of geldings from which cowboys choose their mounts
Riata	(Spanish), Var. reata - Braided rawhide rope favored by cowboys in California, Nevada, and Oregon; commonly called a 'gutline',

	much longer than grass ropes, being from 65 to 125 feet in length
Ribbons	'Lines'; leather straps used to drive horses
Riggin'	Rigging; western saddle
Romal	A single braided strap with a popper on one end, attached to braided reins, which is used as an extension or in place of a whip
Rough strings	'Green' or untrained horses that will buck or fight anyone who attempts to ride them
Set horse up	Causing a horse to stop hard on his haunches or brace himself in expectation of a hard jolt, especially from a strong force on the other end of the cowboy's rope
Snub horse	Solid, well built horse, used for hard roping, able to withstand lots of hard jerks
Sunfishing	Bucking; jumping in the air and swapping ends and landing in the opposite direction
Swing team	Center team (pair) of horses in a six-up
Took my turns	To dally; wrapping the rope around the saddle horn two or three times to hold it secure whan a cowboy is roping; Right handers go counter clockwise; left handers the reverse
Trackin'	Moving a horse one or more steps out of his tracks where he stood while being saddled
Wheelers	Horses harnessed just in front of the wheels of a wagon or coach
Woolies	Chaps (pronounced shaps), made of Angora goat or sheepskin having very long hair for cold weather

ABOUT THE ILLUSTRATOR

Margery Wolverton began drawing horses before she entered kindergarten; and continues her love of art work to this day. After being married to Red for more than 50 years, and seeing first hand the western way of life, the illustrations are her attempts to capture some of those moments of the working Cowboys.

Layout, Design, & back cover photo by Wendy L. Wolverton

ABOUT THE AUTHOR

'Red Cloud', as he is known in the cattle country, has been a working cowboy and horseman all his life. Raised on a ranch in Colorado, he quit school at sixteen and went to work breaking mules to drive for the ZX Ranch at Paisley, Oregon, until he got hired on 'with the wagon'. "All I ever wanted to be was a 'big ranch' cowboy. The first 30 years of my life, I didn't know I could make a living if I wasn't ahorseback. I liked punching cows, riding broncs, and driving fast horses. I took part in a stagecoach holdup at a rodeo, which eventually evolved into getting one of my own and breaking 6-up hitches of Morgan horses to pull it. Two of the highlights were our 1976 stagecoach trip from St. Joseph, Missouri to Sacramento, California; and our invitation to President Carter's Inaugural Parade in 1977, representing the 17 western states. We started providing horses for the movies in 1975 with 'White Buffalo'. Been at it ever since, including 'Tombstone', 'The Alamo', and 'Into The West'."

His first published work was the story of the Bi-Centennial stagecoach trip "Stagecoach 76', in 'The Tombstone Epitaph'. His current stories in "The Cowboy" magazine are of his life as a working cowboy.

Red lives with his wife on their horse ranch near Tucson, Arizona.

ISBN 141208338-9

9 781412 083386